Florence Smith, Henry Whitney Bellow

Piero's Painting

And other Poems and Papers

Florence Smith, Henry Whitney Bellow

Piero's Painting
And other Poems and Papers

ISBN/EAN: 9783744767507

Printed in Europe, USA, Canada, Australia, Japan

Cover: Foto ©Andreas Hilbeck / pixelio.de

More available books at **www.hansebooks.com**

A MEMORIAL FOR HER FRIENDS.

PIERO'S PAINTING

AND

OTHER POEMS AND PAPERS,

BY

FLORENCE SMITH.

EDITED

BY HENRY W. BELLOWS,

PASTOR OF ALL SOULS CHURCH, NEW YORK.

PRINTED, NOT PUBLISHED.

NEW YORK:
SCRIBNER, ARMSTRONG & COMPANY,
SUCCESSORS TO
CHARLES SCRIBNER & CO.,
654 BROADWAY.
1872.

POOLE & MACLAUCHLAN, PRINTERS,
205–213 *East Twelfth Street,*
NEW YORK.

PREFACE.

Florence Smith, daughter of Augustus F. Smith and Lucy Elliot, was born in New York, March 11, 1845, and died after a sudden illness, in her father's house at Fort Washington, July 19, 1871.

A brief memorial by her Pastor, published shortly after her decease, and reprinted here, will sufficiently introduce the poems and few prose papers now offered her friends—which may safely be left to make their own impression.

[From the "*Liberal Christian*" of August 10, 1871.]

"The death of this lovely young woman, so lately moving in beauty and promise through the wide circle of her acquaintances, has naturally aroused an intense feeling of sorrow and sympathy. Although slight in frame and delicate in appearance, she had been accustomed to such an earnest and varied life, and was so capable of mental labor and

social activity, that few persons could have imagined her
either frail in constitution or liable to be taken off by sudden
illness. Doubtless the recent loss of a beloved mother and
an aunt almost equally dear (both dying within one month)
had given a dangerous shock to her system. Still more, the
responsibilities of an elder sister, called to take the place of
a most capable and devoted mother, had wrought upon her
serious and conscientious nature with perilous force, and
thinned away her power of resistance, until the assault of
typhoid fever, raging with unaccountable violence in her
system, found no reserved strength there to oppose it. A
few days did the usual work of weeks of sickness in breaking
up her constitution, and she died after being almost during
the whole of her severe illness in an unconscious or delirious
condition. Even in this state her habitual thoughtfulness
for others, sweet submission to pain and distress, and acqui-
escence in the wishes of those in care of her, triumphed
over an enfeebled and wandering mind. She even seemed
to know that her end was approaching, and once breathed,
as if to herself, the words, "There is a haven of rest at hand
after a hard battle." She asked after her sister, and ac-
quiesced in her inevitable absence; breathed the names of

her pastors, and showed the tenderness, dignity, and dutiful ness of her character, even in that state when human responsibleness ceases, and ordinary persons are so often made the very reverse of their proper selves.

"This will not surprise any of those who knew best this self-disciplined, high-toned and accomplished young woman. For although at an age when maturity of powers and finish of character are not expected, there was in her nothing crude, incomplete, or unsettled. Under the inspiration and guidance of a mother only too anxious to secure variety and fulness, thoroughness and harmony in her education, and who had devoted equal attention to her mind and heart, this sensitive and receptive girl, endowed with unusual weight of understanding, with exquisite moral sensibility, and a taste for everything beautiful or artistic, had attained a culture and discipline almost unexampled in women of her years. Exact and thorough in her elementary scholarship; reading with system only the best books; methodical in the storing and order of her mind; devoting certain hours of the day to solitude and study—she had laid up a rare amount of knowledge, and acquired a rarer habit of digesting what she learned into wisdom. To her fine acquirements in English history and literature she had added such a knowledge of German, French, and Italian as enabled her to profit by the classical works in those languages. No difficulties daunted her in coping with anything she wished to acquire. Patient, persistent, courageous, she conquered what might be repug-nant to her aptitudes by the force of her will and the inde-fatigableness of her attention.

"Yet her solid studies had a perpetual rival in her æsthetic taste. She had the temperament of a poet and the disposi-tion of an artist. Sensitive to the beauties of nature, the charms of solitary walks and lonely meditations, she found the banks of the Hudson and the woods of Washington Heights sources of inspiration, and fed her soul upon the ripples of the river, the vistas that let in the morning and evening sky, the budding trees, gay insects and wild flowers, until the divine beauty of God's world had fashioned her spirit into its own loveliness. The feelings thus inspired she could pour out shyly in mellifluous and highly imaginative verse, reserved for the eye of her choicest friends. She celebrated her friendships with the offering of her graceful muse. Had she lived to acquire a little more confidence in her own genius and a little less reserve, we cannot doubt

that she might have taken a public place among the acknow
ledged poetesses of the land. But poetry was not more a
necessity of her nature than pictorial art, which she not
only felt the appetite to enjoy but the longing to create.

" The chief charm of the new Home in New York—
darkened over by the absence of the mother that had ex-
pended so much thoughtfulness and taste in preparing it for
her children—was, for Florence, her own studio, hung about
with her own productions, and where she found a rare
pleasure in applying the knowledge and skill she had dili-
gently sought in the studios of professional artists. The
pencil and the brush, familiar to her hands from an early
age, were every day becoming dearer ; music, too, although
not perhaps the most attractive and easy of the arts to her,
she had mastered to a rare degree, reading classical authors
with a facility, and rendering them with a correctness and
ease, which only the persistency of her unconquerable will
and the habitual thoroughness and aspiration of her nature
could have made possible. Lovely and lofty in person and
bearing, she achieved all that so dignified and spiritually-
minded a girl could have desired in social accomplishments
or successes. Incapable of seeking the vulgar triumphs of

mere beauty, or of using the frivolous arts of thoughtless
men-pleasers, she had gained a place in the admiration, respect, and affections of all refined and competent judges of
womanly charms and worth such as very few girls attain.
With all the celestial delicacy and spiritual expression of a
maiden who has lost nothing of the innocency and freshness
of girlhood, she had the established dignity and weight of an
experienced woman, familiar with the serious problems of
life, schooled in perfect self-control, and settled in sober and
devout principles.

"This was largely due to the essential piety of her nature.
From childhood, aspiring, reverential, and addicted to musing
and meditation, her faith had been cultivated, until in the
strength of it she lived above the world while much in it,
and made her religious convictions and aims a solid and
ever-present part of her daily existence. Her mind was so
reasoning, in spite of its intuitive character, so sensible as
well as sensitive, so largely informed as well as imaginative
and poetic, so strong although so gentle, that her feelings
never ran away in mere sentiment, or exhaled in bright
clouds. What she saw, she heeded and walked by; what
she believed, she lived out; and what she was at any time,

she seemed capable of being at all times. Not without some of the moodiness of the poetic and artistic temperament, she had no moods of action or principle. Steadiness, consistency, settled power, marked her character and influence. The dignity, elevation, and purity of her soul, illuminating her face and informing her carriage, gave her a special place in the respect, we had almost said reverence, of her companions. She seemed almost incapable of descending to the level of girlish pleasantry and nonsense, and can hardly be conceived of as falling below herself even in the intimacies of female friendship. She loved better to discuss some speculative theme in morals, religion, art or literature, than to gossip or chat idly about social trifles. If she did that at all, it must have been in condescension to weaker tastes and humbler capacities.

"Yet her high pursuits and ideals did not dwarf her sense of the importance of ordinary domestic cares and household duties. She had a great idea of a woman's domestic virtues and victories—in the charge of servants, the comfort of the home, the training of growing children, the use of the needle. Indeed, all things that came to her in the holy name of duty were at once accepted

and became dignified. No pleasures, no allurements of
society, no opportunities of improvement, could have torn
her away from any positive duty, however humble its
form or drudging its performance.

" What an ideal is this for a girl born and bred in
luxury, brought up in New York society, who had seen
life at home and abroad, had been courted and admired,
and might have chosen almost any kind of life that
suited her ! Perfection !—intellectual, moral, spiritual perfection !—in attainments, culture, character, had seized
her heart, captivated her imagination, subdued her will,
and became the absorbing passion of her soul ! Nor was
her ideal self-chosen or a form of self-worship. God
Himself, seen in the face of Jesus Christ, was the original,
the inspirer, the ever-present nourisher of the Ideal she pur-
sued. Her own culture was the worship she rendered her
Maker with the conscious purpose of honoring and glori-
fying God. Her faith, inquisitive and rational, was not the
skeptical, shadowy, and sentimental faith of many, but well
grounded in knowledge, deepened by experience, and ripened in prayer ; it was positive and practical and settled for
daily use and daily support. In short, she was a serious,

devout, and consecrated Christian, who had laid hold of "the powers of the world to come," and found them full of peace, comfort, hope, and inspiration. Let others tell what Florence was as a daughter, a sister, a friend: I can only tell what she seemed to me as a pastor, considering her as a woman and a daughter of God.

"Now that this lovely and lofty girl has passed on, we seem all at once to feel that we ought never to have expected her to stay long in this world. A natural vestal, we feel that she fulfilled her mission more completely in dying without any other ties than those to which a maiden is born. And, really, what had this life left to do for her or with her? We could not have wished her changed or other than she was. More would have made her less. She had attained an exceptional kind of perfection. It was her own, unlike that of any other, as her looks were all her own—except in her coffin, where she looked as if her mother had returned to die in her place! Whose eyes opened such a depth of celestial purity; whose brow wore such heavenly calmness; whose hair was touched with such angelic gold, or fell into a purer and more consecrated bosom? Who more than she rebuked by her presence every ill-timed or less dignified thought or feeling? What has this world to offer but descent for those who have attained such snowy heights of character? Heaven opens naturally before footsteps that must sink if they advance further upon earth. God's time is always best. And He has taken our Florence "like a lily in bloom," before its fragrance had lessened, or its petals received one stain, but not before it had opened in all its beauty, and been recognized as among the rarest, sweetest, whitest of flowers !"

POEMS.

PIERO'S PAINTING.

Dedicated to my Cousin Edith, who once asked me to write a story

IN Michael Angelo's house in Florence there is a little room which not everybody enters. There is kept sacred his writing-desk, with some auto-graph verses, and there hangs the picture of a lovely youthful face, golden-haired, with down-dropped lids, simply painted, but a face one never can forget. They call it Vittoria Colonna, but the master never saw his friend till she was long past that early bloom. It was strange and touching to see it there; but, though no one ever told me, I think my "Piero" must have painted it! The story is all my own, except the anecdote of the child's request, which I found in Grimm's "Life."

A TALE of one who lived and loved in Rome ;
Not long, nor sad, although it ends with death—
For all lives touch the River at the last.
The other shore we see not, but I think
This life, though short, could not be wholly sad,
Because an Angel came to end it.   Yes—
If the young eyelids closed from stress of light,
They opened not on darkness afterward !

There is no face in Rome now, like to his,—
My Piero's, whose deep eyes, half light, half gloom,
Shine still upon me through three hundred years ;
No matter where I saw them,—some dim sketch
By Raphael's hand, blurred by an afterthought
Of heavenly babyhood,—but shining so,
Behind the darkness and the dust of years,
Methinks they live yet.   Therefore I, as one
Who knows their story, should not let it die.
   If you could see him as I see him now !
Brown cheeks, sun-touched to crimson, mouth and
      eyes,
Through possibility of sadness, sweet—
Enough ! I told you he was beautiful.
This gift had Nature given him, and one more—
To know her beautiful who gave him this,
And find her beauty out in everything.
'Twas much—yes, truly ! yet men called him poor.
   Down the steep hill where stands the Capitol,
There winds a street where low huts hide their heads,—·
Shells clinging to a wreck of palaces,—
And there dwelt Piero. 'Twas in the old days,
And gardens trailed their glories down the slope,
Where modern Rome now treads with busy feet.

'Twas lovelier then.—There day by day the boy
With his young sister Lucia gathered flowers,
And twisted posies for the dames of Rome.
Light food they needed, slept light sleep, but calm,
And knew no care, nor lived but for the hour.
— A boy I called him, ay! but so much man,
That clouds to children were as storms to him,
And mere warm sunshine filled his veins with flame.
Life's blossom yet was folded in the bud—
It needed but a touch to burst in bloom!
Art ruled in Rome then, and Rome ruled the world.
What wonder if her children stepped as kings,
When Beauty stooped from heaven as handmaiden
To do the bidding of the lowliest,
And princes knelt while beggars were divine—
The crown cast down before the aureole!
Not perfect times those, neither. Let that pass—
I have to do with Art; she much with heaven!
Those were the days of Michael Angelo—
Man, sculptor—who in cool Firenze strove
With life as with the marble, moulding it
By master-strokes to more than mortal. He
On Rome's horizon like a mountain stood,
Not dim, but grand in distance, rugged, vast,

Like that Carrara, which his soul was fain
In hollowing out to set on giant feet,
A mighty statue, frowning on the sea.
So stood he by the Arno.   Raphael,
A rippling lake, that mirrored heaven—and him—
O'erflowing with Italian sunshine, poured
His warm soul forth upon the dazzled world,
And garlanded with flowers the feet of Rome.
The air was steeped in beauty, as those groves,
In fair Sorrento, by the southern sea,
That palpitate with perfume through green gloom,
Dropping their spherèd gold from branches, white
With sprinkled stars—the new Hesperides !
—Mere breath was living then, and life was joy,
Unless transfused by love's more poignant bliss,.
That knows death best, because itself is life !
So lived this one I write of, and so died—
So loved, and therefore, dying, conquered death !
    When the dew faded from the gathered flowers,
And hot noon filled the streets, they wandered forth,
Piero and Lucia, where some shadowed church
Gave back cool echoes to their footsteps.   Dim
With incense, stirring with low organ-swells,
And luminous with dusky bars of light,

'Twas an enchanted air. Far down the aisle
The tapers flickered o'er the altar white,
And a sweet, shadowy maiden-face looked down,
Lit up with sudden glory ; martyred saints
Smiled from the pictured walls and startled them ;
While here and there a kneeling worshipper
Told o'er his beads with downcast eyes, nor recked
Aught of those radiant forms that filled the church,
Down floating from the walls like wreaths of mist !
So passed the mid-day, till the afternoon
Grew golden on the lone Campagna. There,
Beneath some broken archway, grown with vines,
They lay and watched the shadows lengthening,
And over the blue Alban hills the sun
Down-dropping dreamily to his warm couch,
Grown splendid, purple-curtained, in the West.
Then, with the glow upon their faces, turned,
And homeward went, through twilight streets astir.
Sometimes as models in the studios
They spent long days, and listened to the talk
Of artists and young students, grave or gay,
Light chatter : who was fairest at the feast,
What doublet best became Aurelio,
And whether Giulia smiled when Cosmo sighed !

But this was little.   Hours on hours went by,
While silence filled the room—the soft light came
Warm through the curtain, while young Piero stood
With arms uplift, breast bared for piercing, hair
Tossed back from forehead, and deep eyes alight
With mingled pain and rapture, as he deemed
Himself in very truth the hero-saint,
The beautiful Sebastian, waiting death !
As Stephen he had knelt, as David touched
A harp of gold, and dreamed what it might be
To make such music as the poet king,
While he, alas ! so near the strings, was dumb !
So the saints' stories grew familiar things,
Though sacred none the less, and some sweet tales
Of heathen love and longing mixed with them,
Until he had two worlds, and that less near
Was fairest.   Sometimes, with grave, reverent words,
The master talked of Art, whose height supreme
No man might reach this side of all-wise Death.
But who in this life most attained, was he
Whose heart reached for the unattainable !
Some days were broken when the patron came—
Some rich-robed lord, or crimson cardinal—
And praised, or dared to blame the picture ; told

Of the last statue on the Palatine,
Found in the diggings ordered by the Pope—
An emperor's bust, a scornful, conquering god,
Or foam-white Venus of Praxitcles.
Listening behind the master's easel, then
The boy would watch the canvas, growing warm
Beneath the heaped-up touches of the brush,
And strive to ravel out the mingled hues.
Sometimes they spoke of wars or politics,
But that passed by unheeded, till the talk
Fell on some word of Michael Angelo's
To Julius, or the Emperor's answer, made
To taunting courtier : " Dukes are mine,
To make or unmake ; but the artist, God's ! "
Then glanced the tide of converse yet aside
With richly-flowing words, to tell of feasts
In Florence, or of looked-for pomps in Rome,
And so back to the common world again.
    Yet so glowed in his breast the artist-soul,
That all these things had meanings ; and the blare
Of trumpets, and the swaying, measured steps
Of incense-bearers, and the gleam of gold,
And glory of great banners overhead,
Thrilled through him in hot bursts of pulsing life

Only in watching a procession.—Well,
There came a day when some high festival
Had set the city stirring with the morn.
Crowds met in the piazza.   Peasants, priests,
None talked but of the pageant.   I forget
What was the special reason of the pomp—
Perhaps a noble marriage.   This at least
I know—all Rome knew—that the fairest dames,
And proudest from among the splendid court,
Granting unwonted grace, had deigned to shine,
The cynosure to-day of all the show.
      Great stir of rustling garments moved the air,
And murmur of hushed voices, when the noon
Rained down from thousand bells a shower of sound,
And the sharp sunshine smote the air to gold.
On through the streets the gorgeous pageant rolled ;
Wave after wave of music and of light
Rose high, and passed ; while Piero stood athirst,
Waiting and watching, with his kindled eyes
Upraised in expectation, lips apart
With panting, breaths, and careless hands down-
      dropped,
With their sweet burden of forgotten flowers.
He knew not what he looked for, but his heart

Was nigh to breaking with a boding joy.
Life, one long passion for the beautiful,
Struggling within him toward this perfect hour,
Stood up full-statured, stretching out its arms—
Full-blossomed manhood, reaching for its crown.
—Not much, perhaps, to move him, and yet all—
Sound, sight, breath, being—perfectly attuned,
Waiting one touch, divine, invisible,
To find a conscious self in harmony!
So the young lyre, before Apollo woke
The soul that slept within it, must have dreamed,
The gold strings tense with longing—life astir
Beneath the pulsing chords that felt his breath,
Leaping to meet his fiery finger-tips—
Not yet quite music, but the joy of it!
    On swept the stream of color and sweet sound,
Till the flood rose into a dazzling crest
Of blinding white, while uptossed flowers, like spray,
Made rainbows all around.   High o'er the crowd,
Enthronèd on a car of ivory,
Shell-shaped, gold-blazoned, clust'ring in warm shade
Of curtains rose-streaked like the nautilus,
With fair arms wreathed as for the dance, they stood,
Like sea-nymphs bathed in sunrise.   Radiant

Each form, from bright hair, seaweed-garlanded,
To pearly feet, kissed by the floating hem
Of garments shining like the tinted dawn.
So, slowly, twined in swaying harmonies
Of movement that was music, on they came.
A crowd of mimic Tritons danced before,
Blowing their conchs ; while hidden instruments,
Clear pipes, and throbbing viols, choked with joy,
Dissolved their souls, like Cleopatra's pearl,
Filling with perfect beauty Life's full cup,
To overflow in rapture that was pain !
—And Piero stood and waited by the way,
Like that blind one who cried aloud for sight,
When the irradiate Presence, passing by,
Smote his dull orbs with light's presentiment !
It came at last, long looked-for, but not seen—
The joy that should be his for evermore—
Hidden by veiling moisture of dim eyes,
That through the dazzle set a crown of rays
On every head, and saw the crown, no face !
So blazed the splendor on him through quick tears.
    Nearer they came, and clearer grew his sight,
Till close upon him beamed one lovely face,
Fairest amid the fair, and noblest far

Where all were noble. Ay, a queen she seemed,
By the white brow, wreathed with rare hair of gold,
And the pure arch above the regal eyes,
Calm through sweet strength, that could command
    with smiles !
A queen she was, and born to rule all hearts—
Worshipped already—at whose feet the great
Had knelt, should kneel, till one, most great of all,
In after days—her prince and peer—should come,
And lead her forth from flowery paths, to sit
On a pure throne with him, above the world.
Vittoria Colonna, sovereign soul
That dared to claim its equal, dared to love
As angels love, beloved by angels !
A glorious face, yet very woman's too—
With tender lips, within whose dainty curves
Joy nestled dreamily ; proud too, but sweet—
So sweet one wondered if their smile could need
The touch of pain to make it holier.
(That last grace too was hers, but afterward.)
Within the rosy shadow bright she stood,
Like morn's fair star, half hid in veiling mist,
A promise of the glory yet to be !
So broke the dawn upon him through her face.

2

Like mystic Aphrodite, from the sea
Of troubled longing, vague, and vast, and dim,
Where lay a world yet uncreate, she rose—
Beauty from chaos, bringing love.—His heart
Waked with the sudden raising of her lids,
And the sweet pain was life. Somewhat apart
She had been standing, till she felt his look,
And half she stooped to reach the wealth of flowers
He lifted with his trembling hands to hers.
A little flushed before so many eyes,
Yet queenly still, she rose and turned, then smiled;
And while he stood entranced, the spell was sealed
By the sweet sudden magic of her voice.
" *Grazia, son belle*"—some such gracious words,
Sweet Tuscan, nobler in her Roman mouth!
—He went away and loved her. That was all.
What matter if the pageant passed him by,
Leaving him there a moment motionless,
With outstretched arms, as groping for lost light—
Blind? ay! but blind as one who sees the sun,
And having dared to look so high, no more
Sees any brilliancy in earthly bloom,
But that one image floats before his sight,
A haunting glory, dimming the low world!

Back through the crowd with faltering steps he went,
And sought the lowly cabin where he dwelt.
Far from the surging murmur of the streets,
Quiet it was, but lonely nevermore.
One presence filled the air, one silver voice
Made rich the silence, and one lovely face
Startled the sunshine with a sweet surprise.
Still was the house, and bright with afternoon.
Lucia had lingered till the show was past,
Cared for by some kind neighbor.   On the floor
His footsteps echoed strangely, and his breath
Seemed loud there, in the hush that was not calm.
Something had entered and possessed the place,
And, like a subtle scent invisible,
Flooded his senses with a vague delight.
It had come in before him, the new joy,
Transfiguring the old life with sense of change!
—And he sank down, his face between his hands,
O'erwhelmed with a strange languor, while his dream
(If dream it was) worked all its will with him.
Long did he sit there, till the darkness fell,
And the short twilight blossomed into stars ;
Then roused him suddenly at sound of feet,
And a young, joyous voice without the door.

He rose and let the prattling Lucia in,
And smiled, and listened to her merry talk.
But the words seemed to come from far away,
And he smiled absently, with eyes that looked
Beyond into the distance, seeking still
The beauty of that vision he had seen !
From that day forth a shadow filled his life,
Fallen from too much brightness. 'Twas a veil
Between him and the glitter of the world—
Scarce seen of men, and yet it shut him in
Alone—with that one glory of his dream !
One vivid moment leaped up in the past,
And, contradicting earth and time with heaven,
Made an eternal Now of memory !
—One might have called him sorrowful, and yet
Such woe as his was nigh of kin to bliss.
The world around him faded to a dream ;
His dream became a world.   Therein he lived,
Silent among the smiling, although fain
That others should be happy ; but sometimes,
When the gay faces round him had grown grave,
Tired out with too much laughter, his still gaze,
Burning with steady brightness, drew down joy
From heights they knew not of, and smiled indeed)

Tender he was to the fair little one—
His sister, whom he cherished till he died—
But restless at the heart, so that his life,
And e'en his loving cares, grew wearisome.
The days passed slowly, lengthening hour by hour,
Until he scarce was 'ware of day or night,
Nor anything but one great panting pause,
Wherein the whole world seemed to hold its breath ;
Not death, nor sleep, but the strange darkling trance
Wherein life circles slowly, with great wings
Brooding, and from the shadow comes the Birth.
So in a mystery long while he walked,
Encompassed with dull pain, till in his soul
A something stirred, a passionate dumb ache,
That woke one day and cried ; so, finding voice,
The hidden yearning grew the conscious Love.
—Men say there is no love where hope is not.
It is not so—for verily he loved,
This simple youth in Italy that time,
Pouring his soul out at her royal feet,
Who smiled, and then forgot him. Ay, no hope,
But endless longing had he, endless love !
A flame had dropped from heaven upon his heart
As on an altar, burning self away—

On fiery pinions snatching up his life,
To burn, one glory more, amid God's stars.
Ah ! tell me whether in the courts of heaven
The seraphs and the crownèd cherubim,
With rapturous voices tunèd to one hymn,
'Twixt *love* and *worship* know of difference !
'Tis the grand angels nearest to the Throne
That bow the lowest.   Man thinks otherwise.
But to my tale.—There's truth, too, in those words,
So very human : "Without hope, no love !"
There must be some fruition for desire—
Some visible height, beneath the clouds, to climb,
Or aspiration might become despair.
Love is not love till something's born of it.
Therefore this kindling joy that filled his soul
Must find an outlet—though in catching air
It burned him with it ! Shining still, one face
Made a great radiance in him, till at last
He needs must give that beauty to the world.
Not that the world cared—could it ever know
The innermost sweet secret of those eyes,
Into whose depths he looked, as day by day
He strove to paint her portrait ! She did seem
More gracious ever—turning not away

The while he gazed—she even looked again,
Drinking his eyes up into hers.   Almost
At times a faintness seized him, and the brush
Dropped from a hand that trembling did not dare
To give such loveliness an earthly mould !
Before his easel rapt, so passed the days.
His mood grew silent ever, and his sleep
Went from him.   Scarce he touched the simple food
That Lucia brought him—marvelling with wide eyes
At the fair lady with the golden hair,
Whom Piero had such wondrous skill to put
On the rough canvas—that he looked at so !
'Twas like that one in the procession !   Thus
She talked, a childish chatter, falling light
Upon his ears, like babbling foam that comes
Against a shore that trembles at the shock
Of the huge thunderous undertone of waves.
   No more in the fair gardens 'neath the sun
He twined the dewy flowers, no more he went
At evening to the solitary fields
Of the Campagna, where the herdsman's staff
Guided the tinkling flocks to the still fold.
" What's come to Piero ? " asked his bright-eyed
     mates,

Who missed him at the vintage and the dance.
In blue Albano, 'mid the hazy hills,
They plucked the purple grapes, and, crowned with
    leaves,
Sang merry songs with intertwinèd arms,
And kissed the glowing cheeks of sunburnt maids.
" What's come to Piero ? "—Then there grew a talk
About the picture.   'Twas so beautiful
That it could speak, some said—and half they feared
To talk about it.   Very few had seen.
They came away with hushed steps and held breath,
For, faith ! there came a radiance from the hair—
And Piero looked so strangely pale and wild.
Then, Piero was no artist.   Did they know—
Any among the talkers—of a sketch
That he had ever made ?   It was quite true
That he had sat oft in the studios,
And might have caught some trick of color there,
But that would not account.   'Twas something
    strange—
Some magic, that had wrought the wondrous thing !
I tell not what they guessed, but 'twas the truth—
Their words the shadow of it.   From his lips
The color went to brighten hers; his cheeks,

While the blood mantled up in hers, grew pale ;
And while the light went slowly from his eyes,
Those in the picture, 'neath their half-dropped lids,
Needed that shadow, lest you dared not gaze !
So his face faded while the canvas glowed—
And so his life was wrought into his work.
    My tale is almost done.   How long it was
He labored so, while the bright marvellous tints
Grew to unearthly beauty 'neath his hand,
The story saith not—but for him at last
It came—"the fulness of the time"—when death
In one more hour should crown his work—and him !
    O'erworn at last with utter weariness,
He sat before his easel—the strong flame
That until now had lifted up his soul
Grew faint within him—nigh to sink, at last,
In the sad embers of his burnt-out youth.
Full precious were the gifts—myrrh, frankincense,
And balm, and rich red gold—that he did cast
Upon that altar-fire, when life was his,
And hope, and brave ambition, scorning death.
And now, what was there more ?   Yet there did lack
One touch divine to bring the living breath
Into that picture that he loved as life.

Too weak, too weak ! his very heart cried out—
Death hung above him, stifling out the sun—
So dark, so dark ! O God, was this the end ?
" I cannot die ! " he moaned—" Not even this—
Not this for all the life that might have been ?
Give me one moment I can call supreme—
One joy in *this* being perfect, if naught else ! "
He fell upon the floor, and a deep swoon
Held him, with lids too close for the last sleep.
—Yet so behind him Death had closed for aye
The gate of Pain, that grated with harsh bolt,
Leaving him there to wait a little space
Between the anguish and the Silence.—Then,
Within that trance enfolded, came once more
His love, and nearer, till he felt her breath
Upon his face, grown cold with gathering dew
Of the last Night—when heaven shall open up
Its depths on depths of unimagined stars !
She smiled, and he could watch her smile,—so calm,
So strangely calm had grown his heart, the while
She looked on him with passionless pure eyes,
So deep the world seemed sunk in them and lost.
More heavenly was she, and he less afraid !
        He felt a voice about him, though her mouth

Moved not, she was so still. " I know," it said—
" 'Tis much that thou hast given—youth, hope,   .
And young ambition thou didst consecrate
Unto one service—mine, and Love's. Almost
The sacrifice is finished. Wilt thou give
Thy *life* to crown the offering perfect ? Nay—
Look on me once, and speak not. Now farewell.
One hour is given thee before thou die—
One hour—but one—and thou shalt live ! Farewell."
He rose, with a strange calmness on his lips,
Set closely in the wonderful last smile—
And painted silently. No sound was there—
'Twas early morning, and the birds began
To carol, shrilly-sweet, without the door.
He heard them not—he knew not it was dawn,
But in his eyes there stood another Sun—
And his face blazed a moment, ere 'twas white.
—Look, look ! had you forgot the picture ? See,
It stirs—the lips are parting—a quick flush
Runs o'er the forehead like a shadow. Wait !
Those lids are lifting—can it be she breathes ?
No, no ! it was the flutter of the wind
That shook the canvas. It is morn, you know !
Hark ! now the breeze has sunk—'tis very still—

I hear no bird even—ah ! is that his face ?
The ashy veil has fallen—quick, he swoons !
But soft ! a gleam has come into his eyes—
Did you hear nothing ?   'Twas a shuddering sigh,
As when one wakes from sleep—the picture, see—
I dare not look—but I do think she smiled !
" Vittoria ! "—a sudden cry—he falls,
And all is silent, save the piercing pain
That echoes from that joy, too sharp for earth.
Dying, he snatched down victory—dying, too,
He spoke her name, and knew not it was hers !

YEARS passed away, and o'er a quiet grave
The violets blossomed thicker every spring—
Like memory, grown sweeter for past pain !
Yet the short life had almost been forgot,
So long ago it was—when on a day
It chanced that Michael Angelo, being then
In Rome, and old, and drawing near his end,
With slow steps, wrapped in mighty musing, walked
At evening homeward through the narrow street
That led, past gardens, from the Capitol.

Let none dare tell what thoughts were his that day—
What dream of his grand work, already great—
Forever incomplete, yet so sublime—
The world's last Temple, and his monument !
· In that stern lonely heart what thoughts of death,
What memories of life—what yearnings vast
After that heaven, that was to him so deep !
Let none dare tell—for with that mighty soul
Never but one could hold companionship—
His Friend, loved as no woman e'er was loved,
His guide, his counsellor, and worthy all.
Perchance of Her he mused, for she was dead.
Let us be mute—that thought is sacred most !
—So passed he down the steep path silently,
With head a little bent, nor heeding aught
Of passers-by, who whispering pointed out
· With awe the Master—till he was aware
Of a small sudden voice, that broke from lips
Of dainty red, beneath a child's wide eyes,
That gazed, and wondered, yet were not afraid.
" Are you the Messer Michael Angelo ? "
Then with the simple faith that knows no fear,
And "moveth all things," did it speak again.
" It is a long time I have waited, Sir—

Yet I was glad to wait, because I thought
So much about the thing that I would ask—
Yet now I think I am afraid ! Perhaps
You'd make a little picture for me, Sir—
Just standing here—yes, something beautiful ! "
And his eyes shone with hope, and his round cheeks
Dimpled with innocent smiles that came and went.
An answering smile lit up the old man's face,
And the sweet trustful heart made his heart warm.
Together, silent, in the sunny street,
With the slant rays behind them, stood the two—
One looking upward, waiting, somewhat awed,
The other stooping, while upon his knee
He sketched an outline of the lovely thought
The child's eyes waked within him, while he drew.
'Twas a Madonna, and the face was hers,
His own Vittoria's, in heavenly guise,
With the fair Child asleep upon her arm,
While the young, large-eyed John, with gaze intent,
Knelt close beside her, looking in her face—
With this same loving reverent childlikeness.
" Ah, 'tis so like ! " the little one cried out—
" So very like ! and have you seen her then ?
The lady Piero painted long ago,

And loved—though he had seen her only once ?
So long ago it is, my mother scarce
Remembers it—she was so young—but sure
'Tis true, for many people heard of it !
He was my mother's brother, and he died
In painting her.—He loved her, Sir, too much—
My mother said.—Will you not come and see ? "
" Where is it, child ? " the Master said, and went
Where the small footsteps led him, to the house,
And heard the story from the mother's lips,
And saw the picture.   Much his soul was moved,
Seeing her face—so young—whom he had known
Past springtime's flush—most fair, but different !
His eyes grew moist with unaccustomed tears—
Looking upon her, knowing her so loved,
And loving her himself unto the end.
—So the old tender tale of love and death
Was new again, through love that never dies !
   They gave the picture to him.   It is yet
In Florence, where I saw it in his house.

Written between Aug. 4th and Oct. 23d, 1870,
    at Fort Washington and Lenox.

SOME THOUGHTS ABOUT A WORD.

SUGGESTED BY ————————

The Sanskrit name for love is *smara :* it is derived from *smar*, to re-
collect, and the same root has supplied the German *schmerz* pain, and
Eng. *smart.*—MAX MÜLLER, *Science of Language.*

> An amor dolor sit, an dolor amor sit.
> Utrumque nescio—
> Hoc unum sentio,
> Si amor dolor est, jucundus dolor est.
>
> (*From a Latin mystical hymn to the Virgin.*)

" If love be pain, pain, love, I may not guess—
But this I know—
If love be pain, then pain is happiness ! "

So sang the framer of an antique rhyme,
Who long ago
Loved as each dreams he loves for the first time !

For who loves most, remembers : and who weeps
Is less unblest,
That he the memory of loving keeps.

It is a twofold life, part joy, part pain—
       This sweet unrest
That we name Love, nor, naming, call in vain.

Where present joy and absent longing meet,
       Ah ! who can tell—
While each without the other were less sweet.

Pale Memory treasures what warm lips may miss—
       He loves not well
Who loves no longer than the parting kiss !

And what is sorrow's sting—the pain of tears,
       The burdened sigh ?
'Tis to remember dead hopes turned to fears.

The present is not all of love, nor yet
       Can sorrow die
Till those, at last, who suffer may forget !

The poets dreamed of Lethe in old days,
       But older still
Those wise word-framers, singing without praise,
3

Who, taught by life what sages cannot teach,
    With gold did fill
This casket in the treasure-house of speech—

This strange old word in a forgotten tongue,
    That echoed wide,
Till nations caught the scattered notes it rung—

Scarce knowing how the great half-truths to blend,
    Till souls are tried,
And Pain and Memory in Love shall end!

April 11, 1870.

SONNET
.

On the blossoming of a certain bed of white flowers.

ON a cold Autumn day of clouds and wind,
  With hearts too full for tears, we clasped again
  Our withered flowers: the ground was soft with
    rain,
And the brown sod with grass roots intertwined,

Upturned, lay waiting till we should unbind
  Our cherished wreaths, and with the late-sown
    grain
  Lay them to sleep beside our buried pain,
Not lost, but hidden, though our eyes were blind !
  Together tenderly we laid them there,
Cross, harp, and crown, and near, Hope's symbol
    sure—
  In the dark earth the blossoms looked so fair ;
Dead though we knew them, yet they *must* endure !
And when Spring came at last, with quick'ning breath,
Our lilies rose again—Life bloomed from Death !
May, 1871.

CARISSIMA ZIA MIA CON UN ANGIOLO— DA CORREGGIO.

SOMETIMES the muse has looked on me,
  And smiled a little, giving grace,
With some short rhymings, sweet or sad,
  To do her honor for a space.

Some days I dream that I can sing,
  And yet some notes I dare not touch,
With lips so little used to art,
  Lest where I love I praise too much.

So now I'll e'en be silent, dear !
  Some words are sweetest left unsaid ;
But if you want the song some day,
  —I've sent an angel, see ! instead.

"FIRENZE."

Oct. 12, 1870.

———

A BROOK FANTASY.

DID you ever think how a brook must feel ?—
A young little brook that dances and shimmers,
  Leaping and singing down from the hills,
  Hand in hand with a thousand rills ;
Dreamily gliding through forest glimmers ;
  Tossed into sparkles, scattered in spray,
  Struggling now through its rocky way ;
  Silent a moment on edge of the steep,
  Broken and torn in its hurrying leap ;

Spanned by the rainbow, blown by the storm,
Urged by a ceaseless desire for the ocean—
Creeping through cavernous glooms without form,
Thundering, shouting, in joyful commotion,
Onward and downward through shadow and sun :—
Have you thought how 'twould be with the restless
one,
Weary with struggling, weary no less,
Ah me ! with its own light-heartedness—
When it came to a place where it could be still,
Where it need not think of to-day or to-morrow,
But under the tranquil sky fulfil
Its longing with rest, find peace for its sorrow !

With sparkle and spray,
With smiles and tears,
It fashions its way
Mid hopes and fears,
Till the channel, broken by many a stone,
On a sudden strangely has wider grown,
And deep and still, and quiet and cool,
It sinks at last in a mossy pool.
As clear as heaven, it drinks the sky,
Yet dark with a fathomless mystery.

Ah ! the joy that has come to its changeful lot—
Ah ! the peace that it knows, which we know not !
One little brooklet to hold the sun !
A tiny mirror, where every one
Of the great proud trees in the forest space
May stoop, and be glad to see his face !
A lakelet scarce fit for a fairy's boat,
Yet deep in its bosom the white clouds float,
As it were a pearl-built armament.
When the sunset pitches his radiant tent,
What splendors rain down from under his feet !
And where the dark and the twilight meet,
What shimmering glory that grows into stars,
What planet stillness of Venus or Mars,
Sinks deep and is hidden in one still breast,
And the soul grows larger for holding God's rest.
—Just to be still, and wait for heaven !
To open the heart, where all is given—
And midst of the struggle, the toil, the care,
To chance on the calmness unaware—
Oh ! it must be happy to be a brook !

March 27, 1871.

DEDICATION

(not needing to be written).

To my Mother
(who is asleep),
Not in Memory only—not in Hope only—
But in *Love*,
Whose eternal Now embraces both.

Jan. 1, 1871.

————

ILLUSIONS.

LAST night they said all dreams were false—
In my innermost heart I know 'tis true,
And the beautiful endings we fashion out
In the starlight's sheen dissolve with the dew.

I would not tell them what I thought,
Though they asked me, and deemed me wise as
they—
For the night of visions is holier far
Than the harsh, hot gleam of the barren day.

And if to some uplifted hearts,
  In the old tale-telling, the angels came
Whisp'ring sweet words, might they not come now,
  Though they fade when we give them a mortal name?

What though we mourn, we have rejoiced!
  (Ah, the dreams! the dreams that never come true!)
And Youth must still lift its ladder of light,
  Though it rest against naught but the sky's thin blue!

Perhaps the angels wait somewhere,
  That fled so fast at the break of the day—
Perhaps they may give us their blessing yet—
  I say not they will, but they may, they may!

Oct. 27, 1869.

LORE-LEI.

AND do ye mock at me? ye nymphs with clear trans-
    parent eyes,
  Round which fire flickers fitfully, within as cold
  As midnight seas, deep, treacherous, beautiful,
Lit up with phosphorescent gleams of fleeting flaming
    gold!

It is not that I fear you in your scorn—those curling
    lips,
    And the white radiance of the deathly smile ye bear,
    Are terrible, yet I can scorn you, while ye gaze,
And mock me that I lost the crown that ye could
    never wear !

I thrust it from me ! Nay, I.would not keep my hu-
    man soul
    With its crushed power of loving—trembling under-
    neath
    The breath of sweetest memories, shrivelled, scathed
    in pain,
On the hot iron cross changed love in penance chose
    to wreathe !

I could not be as meek as one frail maiden that I
    knew
    So long ago—life has been very long since then—
    Who faded from the world when love and light
    went out,
And ever since has lived a tender thought in hearts
    of men.

I did not love so : nor as she died had I power to die,
   But needs must live — the sweetness in my own
      heart turned
   To bitterness — must crush from other hearts the
      fragrance out
To make one draught of bitter sweet to cool my lips
   that burned.

From loving one too much at last I learned the way
   to hate,
   And, craving your malignant beauty, gave my
      soul,
   That, naught of spirit mingling with the passionate
      blood,
I might burn men to ashes with a love beyond
   control.

Why do ye mock me, pointing with white, tossing,
   shadowy arms,
   From your foam-girdled seats upon the gray harsh
      shore ?
Ye cannot envy me the beauty that ye gave,
Dark with the shadow of the human woe that went
   before ?

Yet know, that while I died to heaven to save earth's
    span of pain,
You, that have never suffered, I can dare despise—
The crown I wore, and lost, has scarred my brow
    too deep,
Not to have left the memory of its radiance in my
    eyes !

Cold lips, deceiving with mysterious smiles, so slow,
    so sweet—
Cold voices, merciless in your perfection, tuned
To break the heart with longing—cold soft hands
    that clasp
Cold arms that cling like winding snakes, embracing
    but to wound—
I am your sister

                  (*Unfinished.*)

Feb., 1870.

MOON-PHASES

MOST like a thread dropped from a golden curl,
    On the warm breast of evening lies the moon—
The tender crescent sinking with the sun.
    Night after night the twilight's mystic rune

Grows clearer, written in the deep'ning stars.
　Eve after eve the tossing golden spray
From waves of sunset fills the pearly shell
　Left on the shore of heaven by ebbing Day.

—With all sweet names to greet thee are we fain,
　Beautiful with young beauty, past compare !
Men gaze on thee as men look on young Love,
　And smile and say—'Tis verily most fair !

Ah, lovely promise of the midnight's crown !
　Thou mayst not linger—Time, all-ripening One,
To full-orbed passion heaps thy flame-rimmed vase—
　Love's symbol, filled full with the vanished sun !

The crescent rounds into the perfect sphere,
　And rains down glory thro' the flooded skies ;
Earth is transfigured, heaven itself more bright,
　But thou—too lovely for our dazzled eyes !

'Tis what thou shinest on, not thee, we praise—
　Thy veiling radiance is enough for thee !
Lonely in brightness, quenching the faint stars,
　Supreme in thine unshadowed majesty.

It is not that thou art less beautiful, ·
But Earth more glorious—lake and grove and mount
Are part of thee—thou givest all, life, light—
Love's type, self-radiant, self-hidden fount!

August 2, 1870.

HONEYSUCKLE-BREATH.

DOES it come the first time with the warm gold moon,
Or in dreams on a drowsy afternoon
When May is melting away into June,
And the blossom-trees have done snowing?

'Tis the spirit of summer on flying feet,
'Tis a nameless Something, namelessly sweet,
A voiceless music the birds repeat
As they soar and sing—without knowing!

'Tis a vision that vanished and left no trace,
'Tis a kiss without lips—a shadowy face
That Fancy caught smiling—an empty space,
Where we stretch fond arms out for clasping!

And I know it is mine by the love alone,
'Tis a promise—no more—yet 'tis my own,
Fair beyond sight, but I make no moan—
     Can Life's gifts be sweet as Youth's asking ?

In the glimmering night, 'neath the starlight sheen,
With a rustle of fairy wings, I ween,
It hovers the stars and the dark between,
     Till it findeth my window lonely.

Creeping in through the gloom with the silent dew,
It brings the old joy that is always new—
Mine ! mine by that token—and yet to you
     It may be 'twas a perfume only !

June, 1870.

MY STUDIO KEY.

(University Building.)

You poor, dear little, ugly thing—
     How tenderly I put you by !
'Tis but a homely theme to sing—
     I can but smile, and yet I sigh !

This little twisted bit of brass
    I hide away, lest wise eyes see,
Is poetry now, because, alas !
    It wears the charm of Memory—

It tells of hours in restless days,
    Cool, calm amid the city's din—
Of open paths down shady ways,
    Where who "loved much" might enter in.

It set the magic portals wide
    Through which, a child, I looked and yearned —
Art smiled, and called me to her side,
    And touched my brow with lips that burned !

And by the fiery chrism sealed,
    I am her own, though worlds should part—
The beauty has been once revealed,
    It cannot die, while lives my heart !

When shall I worship as I would ?
    Is life too short for what we dream ?
Ay !—and the humblest work is good,
    Judged by the thing we are, not seem !

The old, sweet thoughts ! their echo falls
　　Down the gray aisles, remembered well—
Past the blank doors, through silent halls,
　　The sweet heart-murmurs sink and swell.

Ah ! life has many a closèd door
　　We pass unheeding, dare not ope :—
" Faint light ! " we say, and long for more—
　　Faint heart it is, that lacketh Hope.

Tiny magician, teach me still !
　　My path grew bright at thy meek touch.
One unbarred door dim life could fill
　　With happiness almost too much !

Ah, be the lowly lesson mine !
　　—'Tis naught to others, much to me—
" Patient in hope," those words divine
　　Have turned to gold my studio key !

Fort Washington, *May 2,* 1870.

DEDICATION TO

"RAINBOW SONGS."

(Mamma's Birthday, September 26, 1869.)

O MOTHER-LOVE ! purer than all love else,
Like the white light of heaven, passionless,
Yet blending, by a sympathy divine,
The wayward colors into perfectness.

To thee is nothing hopeless—naught is dark—
The poet's rapture, careless of its pain ;
The maiden's reverie, too sweet, too short ;
The thirst for glory, and death's high disdain ;

The lover's fervor, burnt-out with short life ;
The saint's parched longing in earth's waste for
peace ;
E'en the self-love thou canst but pity, find
In thee their passion ended—in thee cease

Each one to struggle for a separate aim,
And thro' thy perfect self-forgetfulness,
Tuning all other loves to harmony,
Learn that the end of living is to bless !

4

When to the dazzle of the world I woke,
Heaven's light came to me softened in thy smile !
Thine eyes were stars, guiding my soul aright
Through earth's dark paths, that would my feet
beguile.

Through thee I learned to know the higher Love
Of which thou art the type, that ruling serves,
Shining, as doth the sun, on all alike,
Loving who *needs* most, not who most deserves !

Blending the discord of my changing moods,
Thro' darkness and thro' light I feel thy power ;
Thou hast a charm for sorrow, as the sun
Weaves rainbows on the dark woof of the shower.

To thee I bring this faint-hued tracery,
By fancy's loving fingers feebly wrought.
Smile on this too, and in thine own heart find
What deeper beauty underlies my thought !

Sept. 23, 1869, DOBBS FERRY.

RAINBOW SONGS

Red.—I.

THE WARRIOR.

MY love has sent me from the wars—
   My love he is a gallant knight !—
Token of one more shivered lance,
   A scarlet pennon, won in fight.

The vivid scarlet, how it burns
   In the cool shadows of the room !
I hear the clang of hurtling arms,
   I see the warrior's streaming plume !

My true love spurs him through the press—
   He strikes for fame, he strikes for me !
His gallant charger bears him well—
   A noble steed, more noble he !

The dazzle blinds my eyes with tears—
   Away ! these drops but shame my knight !
Is it not strange this idle rag
   Should bring such visions to my sight ?

'Twas told me of a blind old man,
  A minstrel he, to whom in song
All Beauty came, Light's crystal gates
  Being barred to him Life's journey long—

That he translated into sound
  All color, touching it. The Red
Thrilled thro' his pulses in the dark.
  " 'Tis the shrill Trumpet's voice," he said !

—Here 'tis so silent while I dream,
  So lonely while *his* voice I wait—
And yet I hear the battle's din—
  Shrinking, I share the battle's fate.

Ah, how he clasped me for farewell,
  What brave words whispered in my ear !
I hardly trembled then, the flush
  That tinged my cheek was not from fear.

I sped him on his high emprise,
  And now I sit and wait—*not* weep !
No, no ! he gave me all his love—
  I have his honor, too, to keep !

I tied my favor on his helm—
What though the scarlet scarf be stained
As this he sends, lest I forget
Through what hard ways is glory gained !

I live for him, he dies for me—
I share his love, I share his fame.
Shall I not bear a hero heart—
Worthy to wear a hero's name ?

Sept. 7, 1869.

———

RAINBOW SONGS.

Red.—II.

THE WARRIOR.

My love, my life, my own !
Press thy red lips against my cheek—
Kiss back the color—hasten, Sweet !
Thy love, not life, I seek.

But this once more my own !
Breathe into mine thy living breath—
Close, close—ah ! Life is all too sweet,
But glory comes with death.

Ay, 'twas thy scarlet scarf
They used to stanch the wound with—dear !
Thou dost not care I stained it so ?
—My love, my pride, my peer !

Thro' tears thy queenly smile !
And art thou proud I loved thee, Sweet ?
The laurels that I died to win,
Are honored at thy feet !

Ah, Death ! this moment more—
Come, Love, one silent, long, last kiss !
My darling, is the victor's meed
In heaven more sweet than this ?

This rapture is my last—
The earth has naught beyond to give :
While Glory melts in Love's pure flame,
Dying, I only *live !*

SAND'S POINT, L. I.,*Sept.* 11 1869.

RAINBOW SONGS.

Yellow.

THE MISER.

THE beautiful color ! the color of gold !
How it sparkles and burns in the piled up dust !
The poets ! they know not, they never have told
Of the fadeless color, the color of gold—
Of my god, in whom I trust !

Deep down in the earth it winds and creeps—
In her sluggish old veins 'tis the warm rich blood—
The old mother-monster ! how soundly she sleeps !
Come ! nearest her heart, where the strong life leaps—
We drink, we bathe in the flood !

*   *   *   *   *   *

Ah, the far-off days ! was I ever a child ?
—My brain is so dark, and my heart has grown cold.
Those fields, where the golden-eyed buttercups smiled
Long ago—did I love them with heart undefiled ?
Did I seek the flowers for the gold ?

Be still! O thou traitor Remorse, at my heart,
Whining without in the dark at the door—
I know thee, the beggar and thief that thou art,
Lying low at my threshold—I bid thee depart!
        Thou shalt dog my footsteps no more.

Wilt thou bring me the faded flowers of my youth—
With hands full of dead leaves, and lips of lies—
For these shall I yield thee my treasure, in sooth?
Are the buttercup's petals pure gold—say truth!
        Wilt thou coin me the daisy's eyes?

I hate them! the smiling flowers in the sun,
And the yellow smooth rays that they feed on at
        noon—
'Tis the hard cold gold I will have, or none!
Come, pluck me the stars down, one by one,
        Plant me the pale rich moon!

*   *   *   *   *   *

Ah! the mystical seed, it has grown, it has spread!
—But the sharp star-points they are piercing my brow,
And the rosy home-faces grow livid and dead
In the terrible color the fire-blossoms shed—
        I am reaping my harvest in now!

The horrible color—the color of flame !
The hot sun has o'erflowed from his broken urn—
O thou pitiless sky ! wilt thou show me my shame ?
While the cursèd gold clings to my fingers like flame—
And glitters only to burn !

(Begun at Turin—finished at home—CATSKILL, *Aug.*, 1869.)

RAINBOW SONGS.

Green.

THE MAIDEN.

THE Spring has come, with wealth of downy buds,
And promise of sweet Summer in her breath ;
The world wakes dreamily, at bright Hope's touch,
From the pale sleep forgetful men call death.

The faint sun shines down thro' the flickering green,
Here in the shadows, where I love to sit ;
The young leaves flutter, and the breezes blow—
Ah ! Life is sweet, and Hope is half of it !

Dim, lovely fancies, how they come and go—
  Betwixt the sunshine and the April rain !
—What is it that has crept into my heart,
  This vague unrest, that is not wholly pain ?

I shun the dazzle of the smiling sun,
  Half sad—my sadness half a strange delight— ʼ
Hope's flickering pinions fan me like warm breath—
  I would not be more happy, if I might !

Down the dim alleys of the whispering wood,
  Heard I the rustle of approaching feet ?
Ah, Love ! the summer is so near :—not yet !
  Not yet the end—the promise is so sweet !

A little longer in the veilèd light,
  In this sweet lingering doubt 'twixt hope and fear !
Ah ! might I wait thee, Love, forever thus,
  'Mid these first shadows of the early year !

Sept. 3, 1869.

RAINBOW SONGS.

Blue.

THE SAINT.

HOT noon amid the barren sands
In Egypt's silent waste of sepulchres—
Alone, between the stark cliffs and the sun—
In this parched air no breath of being stirs !

Beneath, the river flows, and burns—
A sheet of white-hot gold—while wearily
I turn mine eyes from the dead sultry glare
Toward the cool azure splendors of the sky.

So pure ! so far ! I fain would soar
In the blue depths of that immensity !
I thirst, I languish, till my spirit sinks
Wrapped in the endless calm of that still sea.

Until life's fever frets no more—
Until my sin-stained soul is washen clean,
In that great flood that pours around the Throne,
And passion fades in that pure light serene.

As in that holy perfect blue,
The garish colors of the common day
Dissolve their passionate part, and lose themselves
In the one glory cannot pass away—

So might I utterly forget
This weary earth, and live in Him alone,
Whom through the open sky the prophet saw
" In likeness like unto a *sapphire-stone !* "

Might I but draw the vision down,
With mine own eyes, that look, and long, and wait!
—It floats, it fades, before my aching sense—
Heaven is too deep, the glory is too great !

I am not worthy, Lord—I shrink !
The veiling splendors of the lower Day
Would hide Thee from me—nay, I gaze no more ;
Lips low, eyes darkened in the dust, I pray—

Until the longed-for Shadow comes,
Till Death throws wide the sunset's golden bars—
One more earth-flush ! one passion more ! and then—
Cool night, heaven's calm eternity of stars !

Sept. 25, 1869.

RAINBOW SONGS.

Purple.

THE POET.

PURPLE, the passionate color !
Purple, the color of pain !
I clothe myself in the rapture—
I count the suffering gain !

The sea lies gleaming before me,
Pale in the smile of the sun—
No shadow—all golden and azure—
The joy of the Day has begun !

Throbbing and yearning forever,
With longing unsatisfied, sweet—
Flushed with the pain and the rapture,
Warm at the sun-god's feet—

In the glow and gloom of the evening
The glory is reached—and o'er-past ;
Joy's rose-bloom has ripened to purple—
'Twill fade, but the stars shine at last !

Purple, the passionate color !
Robing the martyr, the king—
Regal in joy and in anguish,
    Life's blossom, with ah ! its sting—

Give me the sovereign color—
I'll suffer, that I may reign !
The poet's moment of rapture
    Is worth the poet's pain !

ITALY, CORNICE ROAD, *Jan.* 8, 1869.

THE RIVER OF THE PAST.

ON the broad and slumbering river—
Ancient, mystery-brooding Nile—
Eating the forgetful lotus,
    Dream we all the while—
    Floating up the stream.

All the present sleeps behind us,
Buried 'neath the tranquil flood ;
While the rippling, whispering waters
    Cool the young warm blood,
    Float we up the stream.

Lethe-like, it folds around us,
  Wave on wave, the river dim,
While, beneath our half-closed eyelids,
  Visions sink and swim,—
    Floating up the stream.

Sailing in a world of shadows,
  Leaving Life and Care behind,
Toward the dead Past's mighty kingdom
  Gliding with the wind,
    Float we up the stream.

Noontide floods the river slowly,
  From his brimming golden urn,
'Neath Cleopatra's silken awnings
  Torrid glances burn—
    Floating up the stream.

And the Old World grows in splendor,
  Nearer with the sinking sun,
As we pass the buried cities—
  Pass them one by one—
    Floating up the stream.

In the sudden tropic twilight,
  Statue-like against the gold,
Stand the palm-trees, dark and lonely,
  Monuments of old—
    Floating up the stream.

Upward toward the solemn temples,
  Carved by *dust*, in living *stone*,
Past Antiquity's dread treasures,
  Toward the dim Unknown,
    Float we up the stream.

'Neath the starlight's dreamy glory—
  Flooding heaven's eternal span—
" Sons of God " that sang together
  At the birth of man,—
    Float we up the stream.

'Tis the mighty tide of ages,
  Flowing on while Time shall last,
And we seek its hidden sources
  In the mystic Past—
    Floating up the stream !

On the Nile, *Feb. 15, 1869.*

THE COLOSSI.

Grim monarchs of the silent plain,
  Seated in motionless, sublime repose,
With faces turned forever toward the dawn,
  With eyes that sleep not, lips that ne'er unclose—

While kingdoms crumble round their thrones,
  In lonely state they keep their ancient seat ;
Time's ocean ebbs and flows, with drifting sands,
  Like the mysterious River at their feet.

The blithe birds sing their morning song
  Where Memnon's voice once rose to greet the sun ;
The shadows lengthen nightly toward the west, .
  The stars shine down, the days pass one by one.

Still side by side they sit, with hands
  Laid idly on their mighty knees of stone—
What thoughts pass through their dim brains, silent
    thus,
  Companions, yet through centuries alone ?
  5

Mourn they their kingdom's vanished might,
  Their broken altars, heaped with dust of death?
Or search they the dread future with blank eyes,—
  Kings, priests, and gods of a forgotten faith?

Rock-hewn, they last while time shall last—
  The hills shall leave their seats as soon as they;
But there is One who brooks no rival thrones,
  And breaks all sceptres at the last great Day.

Mid ruins of a passing world,
  To their slow height those giant forms shall rise;
With solemn steps they move to meet their doom,
  From the dread Presence passing with veiled eyes,

Beneath the gate of an eternal Death
  They enter, and are lost among the shades—
In the dim region of perpetual sighs,
  Where earthly glory, earthly greatness, fades.

THEBES, *Feb.* 23, 1869.

LINES .

Written on approaching Florence, April 28, 1869.

FLORENCE ! the name sounds sweetly to my ear—
Familiar and yet strange ; on dear home lips
'Tis music, and from Tuscan tongues it slips
Like dropping honey, syllabled and clear.

My name, yet not my name !—Myself forgot,
Hither I turn my eager steps, to seek
The air those great ones breathed, whom I, though
   weak,
May follow worshipping, attaining not !

What is there home-like in the flower-girt place ?
Why smiles the Arno, while th' encircling hills
Enwrap me closer, and my spirit thrills
With a vague joy whose springs I cannot trace ?

Oft have I mused on the old glorious time,
When painters drew with pencils dipped in flame ;
When Genius reigned, and tyrants writhed in shame
'Neath Dante's twisted scourge of threefold rhyme.

And, meditating thus, while reverence grew
  To love, and love to self-forgetfulness,
  While Fancy wandered, may my steps no less
Have followed, dreaming, farther than I knew ?

And yet—not so. This is no foreign air,
  That once I breathed, then left, again to roam !
  Thy fragrant breezes whisper, " This is *home* "—
My namesake city, Florence, called the Fair ! "

—Sometimes in music comes a sudden strain,
  'Mid unfamiliar melodies most sweet ;—
  The heart leaps forth the welcome tones to greet,
But its past echo Memory seeks in vain.

New, and yet old, it lingers on the mind
  As with remembered sweetness, and it fills
  The soul with longing for the heavenly hills,
And angel harmonies it left behind.

Perchance 'twas wafted o'er the ocean dim
  That lies beyond the mystery of birth ; -
  And the young spirit, 'mid the songs of earth,
Could not forget the seraph's cradle hymn !

—Whate'er the heart is tuned to is its own,
  And loving, we claim kinship. So I love,
  O land ! whose distant glories thus could move
My heart until, unseen, I deemed thee known !

In other climes *thy* skies have on me smiled—
  The Beautiful to me has borne *thy* name ;
  O city of my heart, thy love I claim—
I am not worthy, but I am thy child !

LINES

Written between Venice and Milan, after seeing Lake Garda and the
distant Alps.

VENICE lay dreaming in the morning light,
Her fairy towers reflected in the wave ;
As the dim islands faded from our sight,
    One backward look we gave—

Then on ! where duty calls, and smiling home
Her arms spreads forth the errant ones to greet !
Dear faces rise beyond the ocean foam,
    And rest and peace are sweet.

But I must leave thee, Italy ! To-day
Thou didst put on thy brightest smiles for me—
Mountain, and lake, and vine-clad valley lay
    Wrapped in an azure sea ;

While, floating in the magic atmosphere,
Like a *mirage* I saw thy beauty rise—
And loveliest as the parting hour drew near,
    Thou didst enchant mine eyes !

Thus in my heart I bear thee, stamped in light,
Thine image leaves me not, where'er I go—
The shimmering lake, the mountains, height o'er height,
    Heaven-crowned with radiant snow.

Those Alps ! whose secrets I shall never see,
In whose blue depths such hidden glories lie—
Like the calm summits of futurity,
    They rise against the sky !

On the horizon of my thought they stand—
A barrier, yet an inspiration too !   .
Beyond those heights there lies a lovelier land
    Than poet ever drew.

Beyond—ah yes ! I linger on the word—
Whate'er of earthly happiness we miss,
Still is the yearning soul more deeply stirred
    By hopes of *future* bliss !

I seek not to attain—I but aspire !
I yearn for joy no fleeting moment gives—
The soul grows great through infinite desire,
    In what it longs for, lives !

May 12, 1869.

HANDEL'S HARPSICHORD

(And an inscription read backwards).

SOUTH KENSINGTON MUSEUM, LONDON.

WHENCE come these vague emotions of the soul,
    Like the invisible airs the wind-harp waking—
From hovering mystery of near angels' wings,
    Perchance their tremulous faint impulse taking ?

I know not why, but in this rich Old World,
    Wandering 'mid relics of a former splendor,
Naught moves me as these broken instruments—
No more to thrill with accents sad or tender !

Life throbbed beneath those silken draperies,
   That hang so near, scarce faded in their glory ;
Valor lent lustre to those arms of steel,
   This gold, these gems, have their unwritten story.

But o'er these strings, now dumb, the poet mused,
   In joy's pure stream was their first utterance chris-
      tened ;
The lover's sorrows sighed among the chords,
   While with bent head, sweet-eyed, the lady listened !

So dreamily I pondered, as to-day,
   By melancholy's nameless sadness smitten,
Down the long-vistaed galleries I saw
   Sic transit gloria mundi, quaintly written,

On the old casing of a harpsichord,
   Grown brown with age, the delicate strings all
      broken,
Wreathed in fantastic tracery ran the words :—
   Two centuries ago my thought was spoken !

" Thus passes all the glory of this world—"
   I stood and gazed, sad, but not heavy-hearted,
For something whispered, " Are these strings all dead,
   Because the soul that stirred them has departed ? "

And yet—the hand is dust that touched these keys,
  The spirit is dissolved in far-off spaces ;
The ears that hearkened then, hear other sounds,
  Another rapture fills the listening faces !

" 'Tis past, all past ! " I said, and speaking paused—
  For while my sad sweet mood I fain would cherish,
Musica donum Dei, sweeter still,
  1 read, and knew God's gifts can never perish !

One word remained at last to crown my thought—
  A name so high that praise is desecration—
The name of one whose mortal fingers touched
  These chords, and in their touch gave consecration.

While *Händel's* spirit lives in glorious sound,
  Can I deem Music dead, or dream of weeping ?
Ah no ! it waits but for the Master's voice—
  The Beautiful dies not, 'tis only sleeping !

June 14, 1869.

SONG.

How pleasant it is that always
    There's somebody older than you—
Some one to pet and caress you,
    Some one to scold you too !

Some one to call you a baby,
    To laugh at you when you're wise ;
Some one to care when you're sorry,
    To kiss the tears from your eyes.

When life has begun to be weary,
    And youth to melt like the dew,
To know, like the little children,
    Somebody's older than you.

The path cannot be so lonely,
    For some one has trod it before ;
The golden gates are the nearer,
    That some one stands at the door !

—I can think of nothing sadder
   Than to feel, when days are few,
There's nobody left to lean on,
   Nobody older than you !

The younger ones may be tender
   To the feeble steps and slow ;
But they can't talk the old times over—
   Alas ! how should they know !

'Tis a romance to them—a wonder
   You were ever a child at play ;
But the dear ones waiting in heaven
   Know it is all as you say.

I know that the great All-Father
   Loves us and the little ones too ;
Keep only child-like hearted—
   Heaven is older than you !

Sept. 24, 1869, Dobbs Ferry.

SPENSER.

THE POET'S POET.

"WHY do I love this Spenser so?"
   My sweet child-poet, crooning dreamy rhymes,
Like the bees' song, mid beds of violets low,
   Far from the echo of the stormy times!

Ask rather why faint-smiling Spring
   Scatters the soul of gladness everywhere;
Ask rather of the birds why they should sing
   At morning, from the pure joy of the air!

Why do wood-lilies grow in May?
   Why bloom the roses sweeter in the sun?
What is the happiness of living—say!
   Come, answer me my questions, every one—

And I will tell you why at noon,
   Drinking the sky in through the flickering leaves,
I lie and listen to the drowsy tune
   That memory with my fancy interweaves—

While legends of the olden time,
  Of peerless knights, and ladies without stain,
Murmured by smiling lips in words that chime,
  Keep music with the pulses of my brain.

Snatches of fairy minstrelsy
  Echo the forest's glimmering shades among ;
Far from the tired-out world I draw more nigh,
  Through Spenser's heart to Nature's, ever young !

  .

Dreams are so sweet !—I dare not think
  Myself into more conscious happiness ;
It is enough for me that I can drink
  Deep at the poet's fount of loveliness ;

That I can kneel where Spenser knelt,
  Bowing his lips to quaff life's current clear—
Love where he loved, and let my dreamings melt
  Into the circle of his wider sphere !

My thoughts are Nature's more than mine ;
  He the child-priest, her pure interpreter,
Who, in the shadow of her inmost shrine,
  Forgetting self, breathes, feels but only her !

The world grows older as it moves—
　Men may be wiser—are their hearts as great?
We have too many reasons for our loves—
　We analyze, we study, not create!

The age of innocence is past—
　It fled with youth, and will return no more!
Unconscious Beauty knows herself at last—
　But is she fairer than she was before?

Ah! let me love the golden days—
　In guileless reverence still my spirit bow.
The "little ones" who know the voice of praise,
　They are the true, the only poets now!

Oct. 29, 1869.

THE SILENT SPHINX.

'MID Egypt's shifting wastes of sand,
　'Neath the blank gaze of the monotonous sun,
Guarding the gates of Silence, she doth stand—
　The ancient, the unutterable One.

What sees she with those great, fixed, open eyes—
  Looking across the desert toward the East ?
What do those still lips, making no replies ?
  Will the dread secret never be released ?

In restless billows round her feet have surged
  The nations, self-devouring in their strife—
Those hollow echoes sleep—still man has urged
  The terrible question, Tell me ! what is Life ?

Dost Thou not know ? Thou, with thy mighty front
  Upreared against the everlasting sky—
Through generations hast thou borne the brunt
  Of Time, yet canst not tell of Destiny ?

Thou sister of the hoary Pyramids !
  Has the Past taught thee nothing—didst thou not,
Watching from underneath thy sleepless lids,
  See the first germs of Man's creative thought ?

Thou know'st his greatness, knowest, too, his guilt,
  His griefs, and near, the chambers of his rest—
He left thee guardian of his tombs, and built
  His temples in the shadow of thy breast.

And yet thou answerest not!—Hast thou not heard
 The aspirations, seen the emptiness?
Art thou so utterly of stone, no word
 Can stir thee to the depths of our distress?

What seal has closed thy lips—that strange wise smile,
 What icy touch its dawning sweetness chilled?
Through centuries of the rising, falling Nile,
 Forever sleeps the Promise unfulfilled?

Ah no! Amid thy vigil—nights and days
 Of solemn brightness, when the world lay bare
Before thy searching, all-embracing gaze—
 Once fell a breathless hush upon the air,

That broke in distant music—swelling soft,
 Till on its rising waves a Star upborne
Kindled the East: the signal flashed aloft,
 And thousand voices heralded the Morn!

What Day had dawned? what Finger on the skies
 Had traced the motto of the heavenly song?
—Awake! blind world, awake! and lift thine eyes—
 Lo, in the East the Answer, waited long!

—And did the revelation pass Thee by ?
  Thee, the All-Wise, whom mortals named All-Great !
Thee, Nature's Self, embodied Mystery,
  Whose Type did the creation antedate !

Ay, to thy heart it pierced ! the Sword of Light
  Flashed from that splendor forth, as from a sheath—
It cleft in sunder the black veils of Night,
  And brake the shrine of Silence underneath —

Shivered the Temple's walls ;—*then* hadst thou found,
  Then, when 'twas given thee, at last, thy voice—
The earth had thrilled, the sky had caught the sound,
  The rocks, and hills, and stars had cried, Rejoice !

Thou mystical Two-Formed One ! earth was thine,
  By the great Lion-strength that crouched and clasped,
And to thy Human higher form divine
  All heaven was possible—hadst thou but grasped

The gift of utterance, that moment when
  The Soul, full-formed, had crowned thee—couldst
    thou bow
Thy haughty front, and render unto men
  The Answer that a Mightier than thou
6

Vouchsafed to human weakness, human pain !
.   While thou wert silent, God was glorified
Through the meek Christ of the Judæan plain ;
The kingdom has passed from thee in thy pride !

Forever dumb ! a curse is on thy lips !
Forever blind ! a blackness smote thine eyes,
When fell the darkness of the dread eclipse
That veiled the mystery of Sacrifice !

———

TO A. L. B.

(On sending her my verses on " THE SILENT SPHINX *").*

My friend ! you asked of me a mighty thing—
Smiling farewell, with sweet words like gold links
To chain me to my promise—saying, " Bring,
And faithfully, the answer of the Sphinx—

The words she whispered soft to you alone,
  List'ning with warm ear at her frozen mouth ! "
I hearkened, but the oracle was stone,
  And the hot simoon swept up from the south,

Blinding and choking, and all things seemed dead.
  What needed it to send me hence so far ?
From the old thrones the kingly Shape has fled,
  Shrouded in dust the ancient glories are ;

The desert has no voice : but not in vain
  The search for Truth, e'en though we find it not—
Weakness is power sometimes, and loss is gain —
  The seeker greater than the thing he sought.

What though Life's problem be as stern as fate ?
  The labyrinth lies open from above—
God's sun illumes the windings intricate—
  We know not where we go, but God is Love.

And in forgetting self, and knowing Him,
  Living for others, gaining but to give,
In our own homes we read the riddle dim—
  We do not live to die, we die to live !

Dec. 7, 1869.

TO A. L. B.

(On her return from Europe and the East, August, 1868.)

IN fairer, yet familiar guise
  I greet thee, fresh from foreign lands !
Once more I read thy earnest eyes,
  Once more we meet with clinging hands.

I listen to thy eager voice,
  Grown richer with its glowing themes—
And in my heart of hearts rejoice
  That one of us has *more* than dreams !

That one of us has trod in truth,
  Where round her feet the elder world
Her torn, but radiant robe of youth
  Trails, splendid, with Art's gems impearled.

That on the shining Midland Sea,
  " Whose waters throb with memories,"
'Neath the warm skies of Italy,
  On Hellas' honey-scented breeze—

In the belovèd Holy Land,
  Or where, amid her ruins vast,
Enshrouded in the desert sand,
  Sleeps Egypt, Mother of the Past;

To thee has come, by land and sea,
  Fruition fair of joy foretold—
Life's Alchemist, Reality,
  Has turned our web of dreams to gold!

And while, O friend, rejoicing so,
  Once more I press thee to my heart,
'Tis sweeter far than all to know
  We grew more near, when far apart!

On hoary mount, in Alpine glen,
  Thou, wandering, felt'st my hand in thine,
And while I mused o'er book and pen.
  From the fair page thy smile would shine.

Together thus we roamed, and stayed—
  In different airs we breathed one breath—
And thus together, unafraid,
  We wait the great Divider, Death!

Upon one upward journey bound,
Together, though apart, we trod—
Through devious ways one path we found—
And, soon or late, it ends in God.

Sept., 1868.

TRANSLATIONS FROM MUSIC.

Nocturnes.

(CHOPIN No. III.)

IN the garden at night ! the air is dank
With the heavy scent of the lily-bank ;
The shrouding mists rise out of the sea—
Is the darkness over the earth, or me ?

I tread the old path, and I stretch my hands
To feel for the clinging jasmine-bands,
That clustered yesterday round Her curls,
With their white, sweet blossoms, fairer than pearls.

They droop, they are trembling under my touch—
Ah, but one step farther.   I ask not much—
Where the faint, crushed rose-leaves kiss my feet,
To die with the Summer, when death is sweet !

In the dim West breaketh a struggling light,
The Love-star is sinking down thro' the night—
My life glides with it out toward the deep.
I am weary with joy—oh, let me sleep !

At twilight she told me, under the vine—
I am hers forever, as she is mine !
We have loved each other—that is best—
Though we died together, she on my breast !

Is there one dark thought to ruffle my dream ?
The midnight feast after, the strange hot gleam
That lit her father's eyes, as he filled
My cup with the red wine until it spilled—

And I drank to him with my voice, by name,
And I drank to her with my heart aflame,
In silence that speaks more loud than breath—
And she drank with me, but we both drank death !

She lieth so still and white in the room—
And I faint out here, in the perfumed gloom ;
Between us there lies the castle wall
I leaped over once—now barriers fall

With the last struggling, human, long-drawn sigh :—
We are drifting together, she and I,
Soul clasped with soul, toward eternity—
The hand that would chain us has set us free !

Ah, the clouds are breaking, 'tis almost dawn—
The fresh breeze comes whispering up from the lawn,
The dew falls cool on valley and hill—
It touches my forehead, and I am still.

Where the roses have fallen, lay me low—
Life's fever-flush over—'tis holier so !
Crown me with lilies, calm after strife—
The passionate perfume exhales with life !

The calm grows deeper—I close my eyes—
Do I hear the heavenly harmonies ?
Joy's undertone through my heart pulsates—
The love is divine that death consecrates !

Peace broods o'er the earth, peace reigns in the sky—
It was Love, to live—'tis Heaven, to die !
—Peace ! upon angels' wings upborne,
In the strange dark hour before the morn !

Nov. 18, 1869.

UNREQUITING.

I CANNOT love thee, but I hold thee dear—
    Thou must not stay—I cannot bid thee go !
I am so lonely, and the end draws near—
    Ah, love me still, but do not tell me so !

'Tis but a little longer—keep thy faith !
    Though love's last rapture I shall never know,
I fain would trust thee, even unto death.
    Ah, love me still, but do not tell me so !

I am so poor I have no self to give,
    And less than *all* I will not offer, no !
I die, but not for thee—fain would I live—
    Ay ! love me still, but do not tell me so !

Like a strange flower that blossoms in the night,
And dies at dawn, love faded long ago—
Born in a dream, it perished with the light—
Lov'st thou me still? ah, do not tell me so!

Let me imagine that thou art my friend—
No less—no more, I ask for here below!
Be patient with me even to the end—
Loving me still, thou wilt not tell me so!

Those words were sweet once—never more again!
—I thought my dream had vanished, let it go!
I dreamed of joy—I woke, it turned to pain—
Ah, love me still, but never tell me so!

I cannot lose thee yet, so near to heaven!
There with diviner love all souls shall glow;
There is no marriage bond, no vows are given—
Thou'lt love me still, nor need to tell me so!

Ah! I am selfish, asking even this—
I cannot love thee, nor yet bid thee go!
To utter love is nigh love's dearest bliss—
Thou lov'st me still, and dost not tell me so!

Dec. 3, 1869.

TO ROSALIE.

*On sending her a bud from a bouquet of roses, which, being absent, she
did not receive, Friday evening, January 14th, 1870.*

AMONG the brilliant faces yester eve,
The rippling voices and the laughter gay,
I knew not what I missed that made me grieve—
My rosebud was not there, queen-flower of the
  bouquet !

Glad were the others, as at other times,
But I, from knowing sweeter might have been,
Was scarce attunèd to the music's chimes,
Nor fain, as oft, to join the dancers' merry din.

Something there was that touched the conscious air
With faint suggestion of thy presence still—
Thy breath, thy smile, were near me everywhere,
As scent of unseen flowers the longing sense may
  thrill.

Perhaps this creamy tinted pile of bloom,
With violets for shadows, that all night
Stood near me, through the dazzle of the room,
Fillèd the void I felt, not *saw*, with vague delight !

The flowers are withered now, and all is past.
They had been lovelier in thy hand, my sweet!
But still the perfume lingers to the last,
As the invisible soul with sense and death doth meet.

The Near is no more ours than the Beyond;
But that fades with the touch, the other lives;
And the Ideal, by a mystic bond
Above, yet one with us, still in withdrawing, gives.

So this, the fragrance of a joy that's fled,
May I still send embalmed in memory;
To living love no absence can make dead;
And though thou know it not, this bud is part of thee!

Jan. 16, 1870.

———

FROM WITHOUT.

AH! let me lie the livelong summer day,
Breathed into, but not breathing—touched and stirred
  By careless sunshine's wandering ray,
    Chance song of bird—

Half waking to the warm wind's soft caress,
Dreaming, while light the velvet-footed hours go by,
    Happy in Nature's happiness,
        Nor knowing why !

No poet am I—though perhaps of such
Who sipped the vintage of immortal youth
    In olden days, and, loving much,
        Knew most of Truth.

I cannot *make* the beauty that I love,
Nor even sing it of my own free will ;
    The glory rains down from above,
        And I lie still.

Like the Æolian harp, that lives alone
In music, and without the wind were dumb,
    I wait a rapture not my own,
        And it will come.

E'en now the viewless power my heart-strings
    sweeps :
I am the harp, heaven sends the melody.
    What breathes ? what stirs the soul that sleeps ?
        The wind—not I.

Feb. 13, 1870.

LINES

Written after reading GEORGE ELIOT'S *" Spanish Gypsy."*

PANTING, oppressed, with aching heart I come
From the dark depths where a pale Genius stands,
Holding with steady hand the heaven-lit torch
Whose light reveals naught but the caverns vast
That wind through endless regions of despair !
A form in woman's garments dressed, but stern
And terrible as some old heathen god
Frozen to marble by a cold-eyed Fate —
A solemn sovereign, there she holds her state.
Crowds bend in homage at her awful shrine,
And gaze with hungry eyes upon the flame,
Sun-bright, she raises in her sceptred hand—
Her kingdom's sign, revealer of her woe.
Down the dim paths the human multitude
Press, eager, till they reach their dazzling goal ;
Then, blind, bewildered, wander aimless on,
And lose themselves forever in the dark.
    From forth those tomb-like vaults, where Hope lies
        dead,
Love suffocates, and Faith has lost her wings,

With lightened breath I come to upper air.
—O God ! the woods are green, the meadows soft ;
The great sea clasps the earth round lovingly ;
Light tips the waves with changing opal glow,
Light glimmers in the forest 'neath the shade,
Light tints the flowers, and on the mountain tops
Sits glorious, and makes them crystal thrones !
Thy thunders crash in brilliancy—Thy clouds
Shed living diamonds on the thirsty earth,
And, far above the changing, rolling world,
The vast concave of space, filled full of Light,
Enwraps the universe with veils of stars !
—And can it be, that darkly-gleaming torch,
That only burned to light a sepulchre,
Claims with the sun divine affinity,
And with its upward flame aspires to Heaven ?
—Like to an eagle, moved with grand unrest,
Beating with mighty wings the trackless air,
But with the piercing orbs all sightless dark—
So Genius, yearning toward the Infinite,
Winged with divine aspiring, helplessly
Struggles toward heaven to seek its kindred sun,
And sinks at last, in aching darkness lost—
Genius, God-gifted, but forgetting God !

Aug. 22, 1868.

RESTLESS.

I THOUGHT I had buried it fathoms deep—
 But it stirs in its sleep, it stirs in its sleep !
The beautiful thing with its angel's eyes—
I have buried it once, and it never shall rise
 With the heart of a fiend for tempting !

I never can go to its grave to weep,
 For it stirs in its sleep, it stirs in its sleep—
The warm tears pierce thro' the piled-up mould,
And they wake with their dropping the ashes cold
 That the grass has long since grown over.

'Neath the years I buried it close and deep,
 But it stirs in its sleep, it stirs in its sleep !
I thought it was hidden beneath the flowers
That once bloomed in the sun of a few short hours
 When I dreamed that I could forget !

The dead love lies buried, my watch I keep
 Lest it stir in its sleep, lest it stir in its sleep—
It died in its innocence, young, so fair !
But 'twould waken with snakes in its golden hair
 And Medusa's talons to rend me !

Sept., 1868.

WÛD-AN-WATHA.

Extract from a joint poem, written with E. J. D., and sent to the Adirondac party, July, 1868.

CONCLUSION.

WELL, they found him, Wûd-an-Watha,
Found him to their hearts' contentment,
For he was a jolly fellow,
Bronzed and ruddy, clothed in bear-skins,
With a breezy voice and greeting,
Strong, and somewhat fierce, but kindly.
Where they sought him there they found him
In the Ad-I-Ron-Dac country,
Where he fled in days long by-gone—
Fled to hide himself from plough-shares,
Mill-wheels, and grass-cutting patents,
Means by men contrived for torture !
Need we wonder that he shunned them
When they sought his hiding-places,
And that when our party sought him,
He rebuffed them with a growling,
As of thunder in the mountains ;

7

Sent his scouts, the teasing black-flies,
His guerrillas, the mosquitoes,
From his haunts to bid them hasten ?
Or that in his wayward moments
He would treat them to adventures—
Hairbreadth 'scapes by Wûd-an-Watha—
Tipping them into the rivers
From the vessel called the Dug-out,
Wetting clothes and spoiling tempers,
Tearing dresses with his brambles ;
And the dainty-footed women,
Shod with shoe surnamed Bal-Mo-Ral,
Sticking in the mud for mischief—
Mud, much like to Lasses Kan-Dee.
But they found him, Wûd-an-Watha,
Found him in his cabin lonely,
Roofed by sky and arched with tree-boughs,
With no walls but flowing streamlets,   '
Flowing, gurgling all around him.
And they learned to love the fellow,
With his wayward, teasing nature,
With his roughness and his shyness.
So at last he bade them kindly
Welcome to his woodland region ;

Showed them pictures, sunlight painted,
Or at night-time sculptured beauties,
Dark and moveless as the woods are
Turned to marble by the moonlight.
And the music that he gave them—
Dare I spoil it in my versing,
Adding words to what was only
Music in its purest essence?
Telling how among the pine-trees,
Wûd-an-Watha's organ splendid,
Sang the wind, and sighed, and rustled,
Made a booming, wailing music—
Telling how the murmuring waters
Rippled, danced, and talked together
In an undertone of sweetness.
But I cannot tell the story,
Save to those who know my hero,
Know and love him in his wildness.
Those who ne'er have been to seek him,
Or have sought him, feeble-hearted,
Those he hates, and treats them roughly,
Naming in contemptuous manner
In his language, Si-Ti-People.
And to those who know and love him,

Love him in his simple wildness,
Need is none to draw his portrait,
For upon their hearts 'tis painted—
Need is none to tell his story,
But they know his secrets wholly,
For *he* told them in the mountains!

Dec. 23, 1868.

————

GOD DEFENDS THE RIGHT.

OUR country is divided and we weep,
But patriots all have risen from their sleep,
Their hearts are strong, their eyes are bright,
Their shout of battle :—God defends the Right!

We may despond—we cannot do so long,
We trust in Him who's stronger than the strong;
We know that He will save us in His might ;
Our cause is righteous : God defends the Right.

Behold! they come, a fratricidal band,
Their mother's blood upon their lifted hand !
Their knees will tremble, and their brows grow white
Before that war-cry :—God defends the Right!

We need not fear.   We do not, we are strong;
We'll surely triumph ; they are in the wrong ;
We'll hope, and trust, and bravely fight the fight,
And win at last, for God defends the Right !

April 30, 1861.

THE WILD ROSE.

"Rose ! by the wayside blooming ;
    Sweet flower, elfin-wild,
Whence cometh all thy beauty,
    Thou fairest Nature's child ?"

The rose blushed and was silent ;
    Then raised her timid eye,
And looked up to the heavens.
    That was her sole reply.

May 31, 1862.

AMY.

RAVEN tresses round her forehead,
Dark eyes closed in peace,
Hands folded on her bosom—
For her all sorrows cease.

Of earth's turmoil she was weary,
She longed to be at rest :
She sleeps now, like an infant
Upon its mother's breast.

She ill could bear the sorrows,
The pains and cares of life ;
And God in mercy took her
Where there's an end of strife.

Place in her hand a lily,
A lily pure and fair,
Its perfume heavenward rising
Like an unuttered prayer.

Of purity meet emblem—
White as the driven snow—
Tis fit that she should bear it
When leaving all below.

For 'tis a holy token
Of pardon and of love.
It images the garments
In which the blessed move.

For her there's now no weeping ;
Tears no more dim her eye !
She wears those robes of glory
And walks with saints on high !

September 20, 1862.

THE BIRTH OF THE OPAL.

A LITTLE stone lay on the ground,
A poor despised stone,
And everywhere, above, around,
The soft air stirred, the sunbeams shone,
And all was light and life.

All lustreless and dark it lay,
Its gaze turned toward the sun.
It longed, down-trodden in the way,
For but one sunbeam, only one,
To rest upon its heart.

It lay there, yearning toward the light,
   Absorbed in one desire :
To be no more enwrapped in night,
   But with baptism of heavenly fire
     To pass from death to life.

The sun went down in brilliant glow,
   All crimson burned the west,
The stone's heart thrilled with joy, and lo !
   The sunset lingered in her breast !
     She lived, a gem of price.

LENOX, *Sept.* 10, 1863.

DUMB MUSIC.

THE night broods o'er the waters, faint and sweet
As scent of blossoms, by the balmy feet
   Of Day, departing, pressed.

The dim young moon sinks slowly through the mist,
Leaving a lingering smile behind, while, list !
   Love-charmed, the wavelets sigh.

My heart throbs with the throbbing waves, and fain
Would flutter upward to yon star—in vain !
 'Tis a caged bird, and dumb

The Beautiful, with fingers touched with fire,
Has swept the chords that tune my spirit's lyre,
 But, thrilling, they are mute.

Oh ! joy, to feel ! Oh ! pain, to songless pant !
This earthly air is close, and I am faint
 For one pure breath from Heaven !

There angel harps stir echoes full and clear ;
There sounds shall wake that slept to human ear,
 And *there* my lyre find voice !

LAKE ONTARIO, *August* 6, 1864.

A VASE OF LILIES.

A CRYSTAL vase, with slender stem,
All clear and sparkling, like a gem ;
 And from its lucent depth
Fair lilies rising, pure as air,
 And sweet as Summer's breath.

Ethereal blooms! they seem to grow
From the transparent stem below,
   Too pure to touch the earth,
And, skyward turning, e'en would claim
   Its cloud-wreaths as their birth.

.

I musing gaze, and, while I dream,
The sun has dropped a wavering gleam
   And lit their foreheads pale,
As saints are crowned by angel hands
   When passed beyond the veil.

And now they glow, all filled with light,
Until, transfigured, heavenly bright,
   Their substance melts away,
And in the glory visions rise—
   Visions more fair than Day.

Cecilia's soul of song, with eyes
Upturned to the melodious skies,
   Meek Agnes' smile of love,—
The martyred saints, who triumphed once,
   Now rest serene above.

In purity they conquered then,
And since, on the abodes of men,
    With pitying smile look down :
And if their lilies now we bear,
    We may attain their crown !

*　　*　　*　　*

Ah ! they are fading, blossoms frail,
But still they leave a ling'ring trail
    Of sweetness on the air,
And so within my soul there rest
    Those visions pure and fair.

Aug. 30, 1864.

DISENCHANTMENT.

By the shore of Life's ocean I linger, and dream
    Dreams, ah ! so surpassingly fair !
While the opaline waters so restlessly gleam,
    And quivers in sunshine the air.

But, entranced while I stand, as my visions arise,
  And wrap me, bewildered, around
In a tissue of sunlight and irident dyes ;
  And fairy-like melodies sound—

The tide has advanced ; a wave breaks at my feet,
  And, sobbing, ebbs back to the deep :
In a shower of tears my imaginings sweet
  Have vanished and left me to weep.

Nov. 2, 1864.

LINES

TO A CHILD,

Standing absorbed before GUIDO's *" Michael and the Dragon."*

(L. S.)

LITTLE one, why fades the smile
That dimpled in thy cheek erewhile ?
What depths are these within thine eyes,
And what the shadowy thoughts that rise
  Within them, gazing rapt ?

That wondrous painting on the wall—
The Arch-Fiend, writhing in his fall,
The Angel, terrible and calm,
God's vengeance in his lifted arm,
    God's pity in his face—

I see it now ; 'tis there the spell
That in thy heart's fresh, limpid well
Has stirred the waters, as the spring
Was ruffled by a spirit's wing
    In the old, holy time.

Gaze not too closely, gentle one !
A little while to play return ;
For soon, ah, soon ! thy soul must feel
The *meaning* of the strife, and steel
    Itself to meet the foe.

Thou canst not always sweetly dream,
Soothed by the rippling, murmuring stream
Thou deemest Life to be.   Ere long
A deeper rhythm will swell its song,
    The brook will near the sea.

Hark to the solem minor strain
Its music melts in!   Joy and pain,
The victor's chant, the mourner's wail,
Come, blended by the ocean gale
    In one grand symphony.

Hush! 'tis Life's harmony I hear!
No purling brook can charm mine ear,
For, though the battling billows roar,
At last, upon the farther shore
    They chime with angel songs.

Dec. 25, 1864.

HIDDEN STARS.

MY soul, where is thy faith?
    God *is*, rest thou in Him!
His glory shineth yet;
    'Tis that thine eyes are dim.

"The sky seems void," thou sayst,
    "That heavenly light beams far;
I could look upward *once*,
    But He has quenched my star."

My soul, look up ! look up !
Worship, unknowing still !
Gaze, till celestial light
Doth all thy being fill !

God hid her in Himself,
As veils the stars the moon ;
Gaze on the greater orb,
Thou'lt see the lesser soon.

As when the crescent fair
Beams in the sunset sky,
Intent we look, nor deem
The star of eve so nigh,

A momentary glance
Reveals the quiv'ring light,
Which, had we sought, were hid
From our too straining sight—

So God would have us fix
Our hearts on Him alone,
And in His glory see
Our loved ones round the throne.

Jan. 1, 1865.

C. A. H.

(*May* 7, 1865).

I HAD a dream last night—a happy dream,
I write it now with tears.   Might I recall
That vision fair, and clasp it to my breast !
—Methought she came, the friend so lately lost,
Came in as bright a guise as last she wore
When we two met—and parted : and we talked,
And looked into each other's eyes, and sweet
Was our communion—strangely sweet, but sad ;
Her eyes burned with a solemn radiance,
And mine grew full of tears, I knew not why,
Save that she seemed far-off, and different.
"Why shouldst thou weep ? " she said, and pressed
        me close
In one long, sweet embrace.   Oh ! I can feel
Her arms about me still, and I do think
It *must* be that her spirit came to mine
When earthly things were hid from me in sleep.
I could not bear such happiness for long,
And so she left me ; but she said : " I came
To tell thee that I love thee still, and *wait !* "

And in a moment, lifting up my eyes,
I saw her in the distance, and her face
Transfigured with the dazzling light that streamed
From a half-opened gateway, where she stood.
—And thus I woke. *Did* I awake in sooth,
Or dream I now that she is dead, and I
Am left to tread alone Life's rugged path
Of hard realities ?—Realities !
Nay, Life's vain phantoms pass, but what we see
With *spiritual* eyes is deathless, real,
And glorious far beyond what tongue can tell.

FT. W., *May* 15, 1865.

———

THE PSYCHE-BIRD.

ONCE through the crystal gates of Paradise—
    That land of snowy mounts and gardens fair,
We dream of, gazing in the sunset skies—
    A little bird strayed forth, all unaware.

8

Afar it flew, and sang its heavenly lays,
  While the harmonious spheres stood dumb to hear,
Until, too faint its weary wings to raise,
  It saw the Earth, an isle of rest, lay near.

And there stood one, with happy, steadfast gaze,
  And thoughts lost in the boundless, blue abyss :
A brow to wear the Poet's wreath of bays,
  A heart to suffer and to love were his.

With rainbow pinions folded round its breast,
  As drops a falling star, it downward slid,
And nestled where it might at last find rest ;
  For in the Poet's heart of hearts 'twas hid.

Thenceforth, thro' all his many wanderings,
  He cherished close and warm that heav'nly guest,
And felt the restless fluttering of its wings,
  While throbbed unuttered music in his breast.

Ofttimes he sang, and, when his song rose high,
  It thrilled with nameless joy the souls of men.
They knew not 'twas a heaven-born melody,
  That sighed to reach its starry home again.

But still the loveliest songs were left unsung,
  For when his heart with highest rapture swelled,
Struggling within he felt, while mute its tongue,
  The home-sick pris'ner that his bosom held.

From heav'n it came, to heav'n it still aspired—
  Within his breast it spread its wings to fly;
But he, whose spirit it had once inspired,
  Cried "No, thou shalt not leave me till I die!".

And when at last the happy moment came,
  And from its mortal part his soul was freed,
That cherished bird spread forth its wings of flame,
  And soared with him, where song is song indeed!
July 8, 1865.

———

THE WATER-LILY.

FAIR Water-Lily, floating calm
  Upon the glassy stream,
Too beautiful for flower of earth—
  Thy birth was in a dream!

For on a balmy summer night,
   In golden days of yore,
Peaceful, as wrapped in slumber sweet,
   Lay sky, and lake, and shore.

And drowsy grew the stars ; but one,
   Arousing in her sleep,
Saw, far below, an image fair
   Reflected in the deep ;

And, smiling, dreamed again of Love.—
   When rose the sun that morn
He kissed the smile-touched wave to life,
   And lo ! the flower was born !

Aug. 12, 1865.

TO A * * * *.

YOU would not tell me, darling,
   But I saw it in your eyes—
As shineth in the brooklet
   The light of summer skies.

The depths that once in shadow
Their treasures hid from sight,
Now flash with living diamonds,
And quiver in the light:

And tho' the brooklet babbles
Its nothing in my ear,
I see the sunlight smiling—
I know your secret, dear !

Dec. 30, 1865.

CRYSTALLIZED MOONLIGHT.

TO-DAY the streets look dreary, but last night
The sky was clear as crystal, and the earth,
Wrapped in a robe of moonlight, glistened white,
And seemed as pure as on its day of birth.

I looked before I slept, and thought—" Alas !
'Twill fade, as dreams fade, with the morn "—but
no !
Not thus that heaven-born loveliness did pass—
But the white moonbeams turned to starry snow !

Like to that dreamy light that floods the skies
Are the fair thoughts to poet-spirits given—
Thoughts that in "wingèd words" do crystallize,
And leave on earth some fleeting trace of heaven !

NEW YORK, *March* 3, 1866.

———

CLARCHEN'S SONG.

From the German of Göthe.

JOYFUL,
And tearful—
In dreaming how blest !
Yearning,
Yet fearful—
In doubt, how distrest !
To the skies now exalted—
To death now thrust down—
The spirit that *loveth*
Is happy alone !

March 21, 1866

A DREAM.

As one who sleeps and dreams a wondrous dream,
Then, starting, wakes, and says: "It was not so!"
But still his thoughts take up the broken thread
And weave it on thro' fitful slumbers, till
The golden tissue is complete, and shames
The glories of the ever-bright'ning Day—
So thro' my life a vision runs, that grows
More beautiful the longer that I live,
Until I know that it alone is Truth,
And I but *dream* while thinking that I *wake*.
  My happy childhood dwelt within a vale,
So sunny, warm, and dewy-fresh, with trees
Of murmurous foliage singing drowsy tunes,
And silver-dropping waves, and velvet turf,
It seemed a cradle fit to sleep a life away.
But round about, grand mountains lifted high
Their snowy pinnacles, that, crowned with light,
Floated in glory 'mid the liquid air.
—O beautiful, O changeless! Thro' my dream
I see ye still, and still your solemn heights—
Celestial, radiant, in eternal calm—

Draw up mine eyes, brimming with yearning tears,
Where fain my feet would follow !—Then, as now,
Such longing filled my soul. I could not rest,
And, all the beauty of that vale forgot,
I set my feet to climb the barren steep.
Painful each step, but still the end in sight,
I climbed unweariedly, till storms arose ;
And whirling gales, and floods, and darkness dire
Blinded mine eyes, and beat me to the ground :
Yet still I struggled on . . . . And now, methinks,
I dream as then, and with my closèd eyes
I see the shadowy shape, that thro' the storm
Hovered above me, robed in shifting white,
Pointing the way, and sometimes bending down
As though to lift me in its cloudy arms.
　　I feared it then, mysterious Messenger !
And, trembling, shrank, as from a cold embrace :
I thought it some dread spectre of the night,
And named it *Death.*—Oh ! ignorant !
For now I know it for an *angel* sent
From heav'n in love to guide my weary feet ;
And what, in vague affright, seemed terrible,
Has grown, with time, to be the dearest hope !
　　And so I tread the stormy path of life,

And as in dream I pass through shade and sun,
With heart still lifted to those heights sublime :
And still the cloud-robed One attends my steps.
From day to day more lovingly he looks,
More radiant his eyes, as sun thro' mist,
The heav'nly light grows nearer—half I wake—
Oh ! vision, leave me not ! Oh ! Angel, come !
Bear me aloft upon thy snowy wings,
Gaze down into my soul with look serene,
And I will close my eyes once more, to wake
Where dreams become reality—in Heaven !

FT. W., *April* 29, 1866.

LINES

With thanks for some wild-flowers.

(H. E.)

COME, tell me, tell me, blossoms fair,
And do ye no sweet message bear
From one who loves me well ?

11

She sends no written word, and yet
This sweetly scented floweret—
    It is not dumb to me.

For *words alone* are hard and cold,
The fervid spirit scarce can mould
    Them into breathing forms.

A look, a tone, a smile, tell more
Of all the heart's strange, hidden lore
    Than many a gilded tome.

A faded flower, whose perfume still
Doth faintly linger, oft will fill
    The heart with mem'ries sweet.

Tho' form and hue are crushed and gone,
The *soul* remains, and still lives on
    More beautiful than they.

Ah, yes! when earthly blooms depart,
There lives a perfume of the heart
    Embalming withered joys!

And so I keep these blossoms fair,
For on their honeyed breath they bear
The love they cannot *tell !*

May 6, 1866.

IN MEMORIAM.

C. S. E.

(*May* 17, 1866.)

OUR dear one, fading from our sight away
Till but a shadow of herself, still kept
Her loving heart, that grew, from day to day,
Thro' pain more loving, till at last she " slept,"

Like some meek blossom, 'neath the heel of Death,
Whose fragrance, richer that 'tis bruised, is given,
So, smilingly, she yielded up her breath,
And, leaving Earth the sweeter, rose to Heaven.

May, 22, 1866.

THE LYRE AND THE CROSS.

(Aspiration and Peace—a Dream by Starlight.)

'Tis a most lovely night ! a night when dreams,
Like summer fire-flies, light with fitful gleam
The dark, mysterious chambers of the soul.
Half dreaming, and half waking, while the stars
Shine thro' my closèd lids into my heart,
And fill it with a shimmering radiance,
Like some calm, glassy lake at eventide,
Two pictures rise before me—both most fair.
   The first a youth with glowing, eloquent eyes,
Pale cheek, and restless mouth, whose smile is sweet—
The sweeter for the sadness underneath.—
The night-wind sighs among the distant pines
With a low, wailing music ; rustling leaves,
The cricket's chirp, and all the nameless sounds
That haunt a summer's night, make melody,
While throbbing perfume fills the pauses in,
And, brimming o'er with happiness, a bird
Trills, in its sleep, a broken roundelay.
—With that same quiv'ring smile, 'twixt joy and pain,

He hearkens, while on high his gaze is fixed ·
Where *Lyra* burns amid a myriad stars.
Deeper and darker, with a troubled gleam
Shooting intensest radiance, beam those eyes,
As lightning glances o'er a storm-tossed sea,
And thus his words break forth: " Oh ! beautiful,
Too beautiful for mortals dumb and deaf !
This glorious harmony of singing spheres
That echoes from thy strings, O heav'nly Harp !
These sweet earth melodies that blend, and flow
Like rippling streams into the billowy sea—
We know them by a broken chord or two
That strike upon our heart-strings—out of tune—
And oft-times make a discord.   Or, if more,
The strained, frail instrument is snapped in twain,
Like to a wind-harp in a hurricane,
And thrills into an ecstasy of death !
Oh ! why these longings unfulfilled ! this strife
Of limitless desire, that breaks in waves
Against the hard and stony shore of Time,
With an unsatisfied murmur ebbing back ?
O God, unloose these trammels, set me free !
This soul within, this spark of heav'nly fire,
Burns thro' the casket where 'tis prisoned up,

11*

And would flame upward, to the Source of Light !"
—Once more the shining of those eyes I see,
Then, in an instant, quenched in tears, they fade,—
One picture vanishes, another comes.

  And this time, Age stands musing 'neath the stars.
With hoary locks, and leaning on a staff,
He gazes upward, lost in peaceful thought :
And though the Lyre still shines, his eyes are fixed
Upon a constellation that but now I see—
A *Cross*, half-veiled beneath a mist of stars.
And now I see it is the self-same face,
But with a wondrous change—the *poet* then,
And *here* but now mergèd into the *saint*—
Both those, and this—the fiery eye not quenched,
But burning like a holy altar-flame ;
The lips closed in such sweet serenity
God's seal seemed set on them, a pledge of peace.—

  Here would I cease, in meditation wrapt,
And read this lesson in the tranquil stars :
" 'Tis vain to struggle with mortality,
And tear the spirit's wings against its cage.
To wait in patience, and with faith endure,
Is, in God's sight, sublime and beautiful.
Sorrow must purify the soul from dross,

And Faith give wings to Aspiration's self,
Before it finds rest in the Infinite.—
The cross must first in lowliness be borne,
And then in triumph shall the Harp resound!"

July 8, 1866.

A ROSEBUD IN A LETTER.

A KISS I'd send thee, dearest one,
  But send a rose instead ;
For kisses fade in letters, love !
  But this is sweet, tho' dead.

This morn I plucked it, bathed in dew,
  Bright as a smile thro' tears :
Now, while I gaze, amid the leaves
  A face more bright appears.

The blushing cheek, the perfumed breath—
  Ah, me ! I thought 'twas you !
. . . Nay, don't be angry, sweet ! methinks
  You'll find the *kiss* there too !

Sept. 19, 1866.

SPRING YEARNINGS.

THRO' Nature breathes some subtle influence
That wakes within the soul a clearer sense
Of the invisible truths that haunt our lives,
And, deeper than the coral-seeker dives
In Indian seas, lie, beautiful and strange,
Far down beneath the passions' ceaseless change.
   Often it seems, in the first days of spring,
As if the very grass were murmuring
A whispered song, mysteriously sweet,
And the brown seeds beneath our careless feet
Say the same language that our souls would speak,
And strive to find the very things we seek.

SONG OF THE SEEDS.

'TIS so dark, so dark here under the ground !
   We reach and we struggle we know not where !
We long for something we have not found,
   We seek and we find not, but cannot despair !

It is warm and sweet here under the earth,
And so peaceful too—why cannot we stay!.
What is this change that is named a *birth* ?
And what is that wonderful thing called the Day ?

But a power is on us : we may not wait ;
Within us we feel it struggle and thrill—
While *upward* we reach to find our fate,
And this ceaseless, mysterious want to fulfil.

They say that at last we shall reach the Air—
Will breathing be freedom, and Light be Life ?
What mystic change shall we meet with there
When the blossom shall crown this mute, strange
strife ?

So, ending answerless, the song is done—
The song so oft upon the earth begun,
Whose closing and triumphant harmonies
Shall ne'er be sounded but beyond the skies.

May 26, 1867.

LINES

Suggested by EDWIN WHITE's *study for a picture of " Fra Angelico
at Prayer."*

GO forth, meek picture ! speak unto the world !
—Thy sober tints refresh, amid the glare—
Go, tell the restless shallow-hearted throng
The story of the artist-monk at prayer.

Mayhap 'twill listen : though the tale be old,
'Tis sweet as faded violets, and will last—
Like the Fra's angels, clad in vestments quaint,
Whose tender, rapturous faces have no Past.

Ah ! might these pictured forms impress the heart,
And this pale, humble figure at the shrine
Draw down upon the age what for himself
He sought, and found—Love's effluence divine !

The world, a Titan, with its hundred hands—
Struck blind by Pride beneath the blaze of noon—
Reaches out wearily, and longs for light
In its own darkness, void of stars or moon.

Restless, unsatisfied,—aspiring ? yes !
But seeking Self—self-hating while it seeks—
To such, a quick'ning fount 'mid desert sands,
This picture, in its pure, cool beauty, speaks.

Oh ! might all learn of him whom Art so blessed !
Might all—the ignorant, faithless, and afraid,
The frail, fame-loving, disappointed, proud—
Know, that before he dared to paint, he prayed !

June 18, 1868.

To A. D.

With a Wedding-Present of a Clock.

GIFTS are the language that we give our love ;
Words perish, but the soul that speaks them, never !
So, Addie ! take my gift, remembering still
This is for *Time*, but friendship lasts forever !

LENOX, *June* 25, 1868.

A SONG

DEDICATED TO L. L.

Suggested by an incident during a country walk.

MY Psyche, with dreamy eyes,
  Half woman, half a child,
Once caught a butterfly by surprise—
  Smiling—nor knowing she smiled !

He hovered about her mouth,
  As 'twere a rosebud red ;
Her breath was the breath of the south,
  Sunshine the hair of her head.

She wooed him not, but he came—
  She knew not she was fair—
But he brushed by her cheek like a flame,
  Leaving the blush-stain there !

Alas ! for the fluttering thing,
  His plumage all despoiled !
Alas ! for the butterfly wing,
  Rainbow-hued once, now so soiled !

But ah ! for the lily-cheek,
Flushed into sudden bloom !
For beauty she thought not to seek,
Ripened through others' doom.

LEBANON, *Aug.* 5, 1868.

12

PROSE.

THE POETRY OF PERFUMES.

IT is better put into prose—yes! Who would
think of making rhyme-cages to hold those evanescent sweetnesses, gilt be the bars ever so finely with
dainty adjective or cunningly twisted metaphor—a
fretwork of shining words to shut in the invisible!
Rhyme the orange-blossom with the rose, the violet
with the mignonette, but let the poetry stay in your
heart, and not scatter its hidden beauty from your
lips, too rude to know under what seal of delicate
kissing petals was solemnized that mystical marriage
of the essences!

Truly, the flowers have secrets that we know not
of, and it is not strange we woo them with murmured
songs to disclose their sweet magic, as the sorcerers
of old crooned rhythmic snatches of cabalistic lore to
evoke the shadows of coming days from their weird
caldron-smoke! Charms of music are always the
most potent—it may be because in every song there
are woven some few threads of the great under-har-

12*

mony that sways the universe into a sympathy of
spheres.   Yes, music, music!   What a panting for
expression stirs through the earth-silences!   What a
longing for the voice!   Strange that perfume, mute
that it is, should have this musical echo ; though the
answer be not in speech, but in yearning!   But this
very perfume—an up-breathing, an aspiration—is the
true flower-utterance, and melts so into the divine
harmony, where waves of sound and sight and breath
mingle their varying chords in a glad sympathy of
life and motion, and the solemn dance of the stars is
its own music!   Yes, perfume is the voice of the
flowers, and they sing their own song amid the mighty
chorus, perhaps the sweeter that no mortal ears can
hear the low pulsing of their harmonious breath !

But for the prose.   Ah, the poetry says so little,
the brilliant words crowd close to hide the meaning,
and claim the admiration for themselves.   Just to
forget the saying for the meaning, or to find the saying that shall forget itself.   Let us be silent, like the
flowers, and breathe, not speak, *living* only, drawing
in strength and beauty, like them, from sun and rain
and warm enwrapping earth, and leaving our songs to
the birds, who were made for melody—not knowing,

ourselves, that in that very breath which we draw lies the great gift of utterance ; that while we think our dumb lives are but receivings, they are also givings. We inhale, but we also exhale,—there is no real living without both, no opening of the soul-corolla to God's glad gifts from heaven, without the answering incense of a perfume—though to the heart that breaks beneath the burdening sweetness of the blessing it be only a longing, forever unexpressed—that offered and accepted prayer !

People do not write much about perfumes. It must be because they *say themselves*. But there are many beautiful things that might be said about them. Alas! all our saying is *about* something— to utter the *thing*, that is what we cannot do. It utters *itself* again : and that is the reason of the creating in separateness—" one glory of the moon, and another of the sun, and another of the stars"—each an individuality, though all the utterance of God : all made by one Word, yet each with its own language. Therefore the Spirit gave many tongues to the apostles by one Divine inbreathing. There is room for all, and a need, moreover, for every one.

Thus high does the theme lead us ; and we cannot,

if we would, draw back from the thoughts that rise like the very perfume that we write of, an aspiring incense toward the throne of the Invisible.

Did you ever think of it before—how beautiful it is, the "offering of a sweet-smelling savor" in the sight of God ? How much it means, this symbol of a silent aspiring, an ascending smoke of sweetness, the essence of a burning heart !

—There is an intoxication in perfume : even while I write, the sprig of honeysuckle I gathered half an hour ago fills the room with its drowsy spiciness, and I can hardly think. I close my eyes, and existence seems merged in one dreamy Now, where being takes the place of doing, and the joy of consciousness, like that trance-like pause between sleeping and waking, is in knowing you are on the verge of the unconscious. I wonder if the Brahmins found their first type of the bliss of annihilation in the over-mastering fragrance of some dream-compelling tropic bloom !

So perfume gives a symbol of two opposites : one a worship which arises out of life, its true essence and aroma, a religion which acknowledges the actual, finding in faith the complement of life, not its substitute ; the other a worship too, but a mystic ecstasy, where prayer is the All, and life and life's work a fading film, obscuring the glory of the unnamable Ideal.

But no more of this now. The lotos-scent is too rich, too subtly sweet—its dreamy atmosphere too irresist- ible. Forgetfulness is not Elysium, spite of the fabled Lethe. Who stoops beside those dark waves, shudders; for then only does he taste the utter deep of Death. Worse a thousand times than the fiery waves of Phle- gethon, the slow-sliding, engulfing blackness of the river of Oblivion !

Thank God we are not heathens, and our heaven shuts not love and memory out !

Thus far the heavy odors of the East have led our wandering imaginations. Poor spirit of staid prose, how vainly wert thou invoked ! Fancy's warm breath, whispering in thine ear, has bewitched thy senses, and vainly dost thou strive to speak in her melodious tongue ! Thou art a sober Western fairy, dwelling in the clovered fields, drinking no richer draughts than the dew distils from clustering sweet-fern or wild eg- lantine ; and claimest for thy domain no crimson wil- derness of Persian roses ! Of such things hast thou heard, perhaps, and in some dainty crystal casket hast beheld the precious drop of attar, the essence from

the crushing of a thousand flowers—a sovereign gift,
truly, the embodied spirit, indestructible, of so many
fleeting lives that died to perpetuate their own sweetness—but thine own is thine own, nevertheless, O
shrinking, tender, veiled genius of the North !

What the world means by perfume is that evident,
substantial thing which can be poured in luscious
drops upon the heavy air, faint with a smoke of
sandal-wood and precious gums, as in Cairo, where
the swarthy Arab, sitting cross-legged in his narrow booth, smiles, and burns for you his dainty
store—myrrh and frankincense for you, and gold for
him—a costly incense before your desiring nostrils,
while the donkeys push past you in the crowded
street, and the motley throng in the bazaar gaze at
your Frankish countenance with curious eyes ! The
air is dim with smoke and slanting sunshine, and
you stand a moment longer, when the shrill bar-
gain is concluded, drinking in with every breath the
seductive atmosphere of the warm South ! But the
air grows stifling after a while, and you are glad to
escape, and seek the shelter of some garden court,
where the cool plash of a fountain soothes the over-
loaded senses, and a faint fragrance of invisible acacia-

blossoms comes and goes with the rising and falling of the breeze. There is a tree near you with a flock of scarlet birds perched on it. Whisht! they do not move, though you stretch out your hand to make them fly. They are only the blossoms of the euphorbia which in our conservatories grows on a low bush, and is even then so splendid. It was a bird with flaming wings, yet songless, and now it is a dazzling flower, but without a fragrance. Breathless, soulless, it is like a tropic noon, crushing life to silence under the intensity of its own acme of existence. It is the hush that comes in the very centre of the tumult of sensation, the inevitable reaction of the extreme. Strange as the contrast may seem, it is but natural that some of the most gorgeous blossoms of the East should have no soul of perfume.

I said the world puts its perfumes into bottles, and labels them, and pours an amber drop upon fine linen, and thinks it has caught the winged charm of sweetness. The world labels many things, and thinks it has got the essences, loves and griefs, tied up in separate parcels, and marked "So much a dose, Miss Mühlbach," "So many drops fine distilled—dangerous—Guy Livingstone"—but the true sentiments are not to be shut up in novel-bindings, nor the pure perfumes to be found among Lubin's extracts. Not to speak of musk and patchouli—vulgar scents—the yellow-covered Braddon type—there is no danger in carrying out the figure. Beautiful as are the delineations of the heart in the plastic hand of genius, there is no poetry to match the aspirations of a single soul, no drama and no romance equal in intensity to life, and art has no possibilities equal to those of *being*.

So we come back to the sweet field-perfumes—that cannot be caught—charm the charmer never so wisely. Their beauty is in their shyness.

THE PROSE EDDA.

April 9. I have been reading lately the Prose Edda, and it is not without awe that, even in so obscure a form, one traces the outline of the primal conception of a God and a religion in the instinct of a race. Like a giant-statue, half-hewn out of a rugged mountain, it stands sublimely in the background of the Scandinavian history, gathering about its head the clouds and thunder ; wrapped in brooding mists one day, another stern and cold against the wind-swept sky ; hoary with snow and bearded with ragged pine, yet flushing sometimes with an evanescent tenderness in the rare glow of sunrise or of sunset. Alas ! now but a heap of senseless stone, overgrown with superstition,· shrouded in decay, crumbled into forgetfulness ; it was once the image of a God,—it breathed once with the inspiration of a faith ! A blind groping, after all, it was, that caught but at the cloudy skirts of His enfolding robe, the universe ; and felt Him for a little while within the mystery ; then, keeping the mystery, lost Him !

13

Ah, so it runs through all the religions of the world ! Many forms, but the same Spirit—many glimpses, and in the end one Revelation. The Spirit is too great for the forms—it shatters them, and overflows them, and casts them utterly away at last, but still some impress lingers on the broken shells of the glorious shaping influence. So may we wander on the shores of a spent ocean, and not unprofitably study the fragments of a forgotten age !

This religion of the Scandinavians, as it is perhaps the grandest, is the saddest of the mythologic dream-weavings of the world. Yet in its very sadness there is something prophetic, and so with a looking-forward and an aspiration, it cannot be all sad ! Wonderfully in both does it show the inner sentiment of a people. These Northerns, from whom we draw some of the most precious drops of our heart-blood ; these wild old Vikings of the seas ; these fair-browed, blond-haired heroes, ice-bound in rock or island fastness through the gloom of tardy winters, with harp and song and feast celebrating past triumphs of adventurous summers, when, with swords for sickles, they reaped a golden harvest from the flashing, perilous waves ; these rough and hardy men, warriors by whom no right of nations was respected, yet lawgivers whose code is the wonder of a later, hardly more perfect civilization; defenders of the poor, respecters of women, steadfast in friendship, implacable in enmity; with a passion for war, and an insatiate thirst for conquest, yet looking with cold blue eyes disdainfully upon the gorgeous luxuries of the seductive South; this strange people, full of contradictions, yet always consistent in the stern virtues of a stoical heroism, struggled, amid the blindness of their northern snows, towards a religion which the symmetrically-minded Greek could scarce conceive, even while, with delicate chiselings of marble and of ivory and gold, he strove to fashion out an image of the Thunderer. In clear-cut, classic verse he shapes a temple to his pleasure-loving gods, and men admire the columns and the architraves, but enter to find an emptiness! Only by the yearning, mournful music of the hidden " chorus " do we know there *was* a worship, do we believe must have been—once indwelling—the shadow of a God!

This other, too, is fallen—this mightily-conceived ideal of which I speak, but it is a grand ruin still, and I propose to linger for a while among its lonely arches, and in the pale Northern moonlight, cloud-disturbed,

to watch the flitting of some ghostly shape, and re-
people for ·a time the hollow-sounding vistas of the
Past.

The race of Æsir, strong and brave and beautiful,
ruling within the golden halls of Asgard, the shadowy
Giant-brood, lurking in cavernous glooms of the
abyss ; the heroes gathering with joyful clangor of
arms in shield-roofed, glittering Walhalla ; the struggling earth-nations, over whose crimson battle-fields
hover the dark Valkyrior, choosing whose shall be the
souls of the slain ; the elf-world, whose transparent
mystery envelops all with a permeating consciousness
of spirituality ; these vast, vague peoplings of the
universe are at one with the grandeur of the cosmo-
gony.

A shadowy abyss, "full of whirlwinds and fleeting
mists ; " a darkness lit up by " sparks and flakes of
fire," a clangor of confused and mighty sounds, echo-
ing as from a whirlpool-caldron underneath—this is
chaos. Twelve rivers flow from the shadowy region—
one, " the resounding," pouring its dark waves past
the gate of the abode of death. By some mysterious
dividing force, the frozen vapors gather toward a
vague, vast, gloom-encompassed North ; on the other

verge there stands a flaming, radiant region, and between, a space " as calm and light as wind-still air."
Concerning this fiery kingdom which stands without
the cosmogóny—" *First of all*, there was in the southern sphere the world called Muspell "—we have no
explanation—we cannot go behind its fiery veil,
" none can enter but those whose home is there."
Even this mighty mythologic intuition dared not pene-
trate into the darkness of the Genesis, when as yet
Light was not—and the Hebrew Moses only knew
and told of that sublime first birth of Creation,
when " the Spirit of God moved upon the face of the
waters, and God said, Let there be light, and there
was light."

But here in the Edda, " at the beginning," which
was not a beginning, we have the foreshadowing of an
end—which is not an end ! For with a flaming fal-
chion sits at the entrance of this dazzling impenetrable
region a dark shape, who waits and lowers, till in the
" Twilight " of destruction he shall issue forth to com-
bat, and before him shall fall the vanquished armies
of the gods, and the shattered fragments of a universe
in flames ! But of this again. From the meeting of
opposing forces, in the first drops of condensing vapor,
13*

comes forth the germ—then the gigantic Power personified—of Nature ; in the form of Ymir, father of
the giant-brood, crouching their huge limbs, swathed
in frost and darkness, in the hidden places of the universe.   This Ymir, from whose bones the earth was
fashioned, whose blood furnished forth the sea, as he
fell with his mighty bulk, slain by the arrows of " the
blithe gods," into the abysmal deep wherein floated
the first shadow of a creation—is he not with his offspring the embodiment of the material forces, subdued
by the spiritual, indeed, but mighty even when vanquished, and underlying the visible world-forms with
a power not less great for being obscure?   They have
a great charm for the imagination—these old monsters
lurking in mysterious depths of confusion and of
nothingness, their huge limbs, formless and vast as
chaos, instinct with a half-conscious vitality, the more
tremendous that it is unexercised :—Strange primeval
stirrings of the elemental life-essence !   Unshapen,
immense, inexplicable, they lie at the bottom of the
bottomless, bound with the chains of sleep.   Like the
wolf Fenrir, one of their mighty brood, conquered, yet
not overcome, they wait for the time which shall
break the fetter woven of silence, " smooth and soft

as a silken string," yet strong with the strength of the god-like.

The old story—the evil and the good in contest, Nature and Divinity at war. Here there is no reconciliation—strife to the bitter end—a purification, dimly dreamed of, yet " so as by fire "—a new heavens and a new earth to come—but what a vast destruction ! A religion of war :—there is but one religion of peace ! And, in that, matter and mind are not at variance, body and spirit are as one, joined, not severed, in the holy bond of being ! Ah, I fear me much that there are many heathens among us still !

But to return. In this sketch of mine, where I draw the *shadows* first, there must be mention made of Loki, the deceiver, and of his terrible offspring, Fenrir, Hela, and the Midgard serpent. His name means Light, or rather Flame—strange likeness this to the Lucifer myth. Beautiful, yet sad ! The genius of evil is but fallen light— the Son of the Morning becomes the leader of the hosts of darkness ! The brothers of Loki are the Destroyer, and the Death-blind. By his wife, Foreboding Anguish, he has three children, of whom the monster-serpent, encircling the world, is one ; another, Fenrir, the " dwel-

ler in the abyss; and the third is Hela, or Death."
Her hall is the Wide-Storming ; Hunger is her table ;
Starvation, her knife ; Delay, her man ; Slowness,
her maid ; Precipice, her threshold ; and Burning Anguish, the hangings of her bed. The one half of her
body is livid, the other half the color of human flesh.
She may therefore easily be recognized, the more so,
as she is of a dreadfully stern and grim countenance.
So runs the Edda, in its quaint and terrible simpli-
city.

Gladly turn we from the gloomy Niflheim to the
shining-roofed Asgard, where dwell the glorious race
of Æsir, with Odin, the All-Father. He, the King
and Leader of Armies, "who bindeth together all
things," "on whom all things depend," sits aloft in
his golden mansion, and from his throne seeth all
things, and, looking, comprehends !

"What is the way from earth to heaven ?" asks
the wandering mortal, to whom in the allegory all the
marvellous tale of gods and men is told. "Knowest
thou not that ? simple is it to answer ! Bifröst, the
rainbow !" A slender bridge, thou thinkest ; but
strong, for over it the gods ride daily to judgment,
with a trampling of many-footed steeds. Thor, only,

rides not. His lightning-shod courser would break the
tremulous arch, and scatter with fierce hoofs the deli-
cately-woven hues into a tempestuous cloud of angry
sparks. Cunningly-built it is, and strong, this threefold bridge of light, and with the crimson flaming of
its deepest fire, it burns impassable to all save the
profane feet of the giants—those of heavenly origin.

The meeting-place of the gods is under the ash
Iggdrasyl. The mystic tree of existence has three
roots, one penetrating to the abode of death. Under
this raves unceasingly the "clanging whirlpool" of
the gulf of chaos. A shapeless, shadowy monster,
Nidhögg, gnaws at this root, and a venomous cluster
of serpents hangs about it, striving to destroy the un-
destroyable. The Tree of Life rises above all enemies
victorious, with the "splendor of its verdure" un-
harmed, even in the midst of the last consuming, and
shall outlive the gods! The principle of Life, im-
perishable, ever vernal, draws its substance even from
death, and evolves a glory and a beauty from darkness and horror and confusion.

The second root is over the abode of the Frost-
Giants, and is fed by Mimir's well, the fount of Wisdom. Here, amid the vast hidden powers of Nature,

the Tree of Life drinks deep of the secret source of
knowledge. Wisdom, underneath the elements, an
ever-living spring, supplying sustenance to Life itself—
it is a grand idea! The ancient Mimir sits beside the
well and quaffs daily of its waters—gray-beard oracle
of the gods! There is a myth that Odin came once
to the wisdom fount! and desired a draught, but none
could he have till one of his eyes was left in pledge
for it. Therefore at the bottom of this well lies one
of the eyes of the All-seeing. What a brightness
there must be there, shining up out of soundless depth
of dark—and what a divine drink that must be, in
which was dissolved that mystic treasure—a richer
than Cleopatra's pearl!

Up to heaven reaches the third root of Iggdrasyl,
over the holy Urdar fount, where sit the three Norns,
who fix the lifetime of all men. Daily they sprinkle
the tree of Life with water from the fountain of Eternity, and it sheds the moisture down in clear-dropping
dew upon the dales of earth.

FROM A LETTER

TO A. L. B.

—So you are reading Swedenborg? I am glad you told me, because you know how I was fascinated by the glimpse of Symbolism that came across me last winter. And yet you have read him first! Perhaps I had better not, now; for although I don't expect to believe in him, I shrink a little from being disenchanted. I have a sort of ideal Swedenborg in my mind, built up, perhaps, out of my book of "Colors," and I am a little afraid of a ray of sober sunshine! He would never be a seer for me, but I should like to fancy him a seer, in some part, for himself! Certainly there are wonderful analogies in nature, *figures of speech*, whereby day and night "show knowledge" to the mind that seizes the inner meanings. Things that seem utterly material, so often by a poetic flash become endowed with a life all spirit—the lower turning into a symbol of the higher, no more itself, but the expression of an infinite truth. And it is very natural, when we feel so vividly sometimes these har-

monics of Nature, wherein body and soul have a re-
ciprocal life, to look for a soul in every form, inani-
mate or not, forcing the intellect to accept one always,
whether the intentions do or not. When we know
that there is a divine unity between the creation and
the creating Mind, we are not satisfied without seeking the interpretations to all these material things.
The difficulty lies, I think, in supposing we can do it
by a definite effort. The revelation comes from the
spirit, which illumines the physical types; but if we
keep looking at the types, by-and-by they will become
meaningless. It is the difference between metaphor
and mythology—first the poetic form of an idea, afterward the idea materialized into a form. That is the
danger. The fascination of "correspondence" as an
article of faith, is that it makes a religion out of
poetry; and who that has felt the poetry there is in
religion, can be indifferent to this form of enthusiasm?
The wonderful *interweavings* of the universe, material
and mental, what glorious harmonies they make to
those who can understand them! What glimpses we
have of meanings, and what joyful seasons of accep-
tation of the low things for the sake of the higher
beauty which is in all, and seen through which nothing

is common or unclean ! But religion includes all this, and more : it is principle and faith, as well as intention and enthusiasm.

July 24, 1870.

MY CREED.

IT happens that I have not always the privilege of going to the church that I love, and therefore, as last Sunday, I often hear a sermon without a word in it with which I can agree, except the " Dearly beloved brethren" at the beginning, and " To the grace of God" at the end of the usual short Episcopal discourse. There is a great deal in those words, is there not? you say,—and so there is—the beginning and the ending—love to God and love to man—which first, which last, we care not, for perfect love is like eternity, an all-embracing circle ! So I take my text sometimes from behind the sermon, and even out of what may not be earnest, make an earnestness for myself, perchance, by searching, finding something of true harmony in what seems incomplete, and some-

times even discordant. If I could do it always! But
that I do not, is my own fault; the "complementary
notes" are not sensitive enough. It has seemed to
me, ever since I knew it, to be one of the most sug-
gestive and beautiful truths of science, that every
note we strike in music bears with it its full chord,
veiled in the responsive thrillings of the other un-
touched but necessary strings. God leaves nothing
incomplete, even if we do; but, ah! how long we took
even to find that out, among the other truths that
continually shadow forth the infinite harmony! and
how hard it is for us to hear those undertones, even
while we know they are there.

Well, this day I speak of, there was some earnestness in the preacher's voice, and some liberality in his
views—a little eloquence, too, but that was when
he was stating an argument for his opponents, and un-
awares the truthfulness of the words he was using
entered into and uplifted him. He spoke of Creed,
that much-vexed question, and though he settled the
matter to his own satisfaction in tying himself down to
established formula, by daring to open the subject he
showed he thought it had two sides, a most dangerous
admission for one who held his only safety in being

pledged to either. He said, indeed, that truth is too
large for creed, that dogma fetters it, and that the divine depths of religion are too profound for any plum-
met of reason-weighed words. He said that the
things of the Spirit are not to be handled—"eye hath
not seen, nor hath ear heard." He declared the danger (how insidious we know) of the "letter that
killeth," absorbing from the tree of truth the very sap,
and crushing in a perfidious embrace the source of its
own life, which it hides at last in the specious beauty
of its own luxuriant and noxious growth. But after a
glance thus at the arguments of his adversaries, leaving behind a very lion in the path, he returned to the
defence of his own position, and here too he touched
on truth. Like Christian on his way to the house of
the Interpreter, he found *two* lions in the way.
Guarding their opposite sides they stood, each ready
to spring on the other, and woe to the unwary travel-
ler who, without the sacred Name on his forehead and
his heart, should fail to boldly press between and find
them chained !—Strange, that in the whole of the sermon the name of Christ should not have been once·
mentioned, except as part of a scheme of salvation
unalterable in any jot or tittle from the iron formula

of an unbending creed !—A truth on that side, too,
there is, though it is harder for us to realize it, who
know not, blinded by the dust of the battle, when our
adversary is forced to his knees for mercy, and forget
that having once acknowledged defeat, he may win
his battles too, like other men.   Truth wages no war
à l'outrance against anything but wickedness.   The
wrong heart needs the baptism of blood for cleansing ;
the erring mind is purified more easily.   Many are
the arguments, and strong ones too, in defence of
doctrinal statement, and much is to be said in favor
of applying to religion the rules that make available
all other forces in the economy of life.   Indeed, how
can we do without some condensation of the floating
thoughts, the atmospheres of sentiment, that enwrap
our universe of would-be action ?   Is not the vapor
of heaven's own clouds imprisoned in our engines that
steam may do its work ?   We enclose the lightning in
a rope of wires, that nation may speak to nation across
the sea, and we utilize by compression the imponderable forces.   Is religion the only thing that is imprac-
tical ?   Is the greatest force the only one that can
never be made available ?   Is there an exception to be
made here to the great analogy of existence, and that

alone to be unapprehended which needs but to be
grasped to shake the world? There must be something to take hold of, some vessel, crystal-clear it may
be, and perchance of no mortal mould, but some vessel wherein this impalpable, imponderable, all-per-
meating Principle may be contained and passed from
lip to lip through the waiting multitude, athirst for
life. Either fold our hands, and let who will perish,
or go forth into the fields ready for the harvest, each
with his instrument ready sharpened in his hand for
no indolent reaping. Every soldier in the army of
the Lord has his arms *given him*, and trusts to no
snatched-up weapon of his own contriving. But do
you think that in the " sword of the Spirit " I would
figure any human-forged dogma, welded in the heat
of controversy by even saintly warrior? No! and
here I come to the point of my discourse. I wanted
to preach myself, that day, though my untutor'd
tongue would have faltered in the utterance of that
which filled my soul to overflowing. One word
would solve the problem, would bring unity out of
the differences, would link together the extremes that
jarred, by bringing in the centre truth without which
either remains forever incomplete. So simple and yet

11

so difficult, so close to every one of us, and yet
so far above the highest ! The lowliest men appre-
hend it, and the mightiest pass it by. But how can
it be possible that this perfect solution should not be
acknowledged as the true one by the mind, even
before it is accepted by the heart ? On one side the
unuttered conception of abstract Truth and Right, a
divinity without a temple, the Unknown God to whom
the heathens raised an altar, beyond knowledge, out-
side of love, serene, resplendent, all-surrounding but
unapproachable, all-pervading but intangible, the
perfect Purity unto which none can reach forth but
the unstained hands, the perfect Light upon which
none can gaze unblenching but the eagle vision.
Through the dark valley how are we to gain this
height of contemplation—through the dimness and
the soil of this lower atmosphere how find the upward-
leading path without a guide ? Humanity cries out
from underneath the shadow of death, and is told, with
" the darkness of blackness " on its fainting eyes, that
the eternal Sun still shines, the God of Nature
reigns, and He is just !—And now there come the
armies of the sects. The old philosophy, with its
glorious intuitions, is thrust aside, and dogmatism

stifles Truth in unending involutions of creed. Let me not smile at the cast-off disguises, now but a heap of brittle husks, which once held food for angels! There is everywhere a murmuring and a rustling as of new life springing forth out of old forms, and the outgrown débris lie like shells on the shore of Time's great ocean, to mark what has been, while we dream what may be. A glory is coming, greater than the past : the old battles have been fought, the old armor has been laid aside. Reverently let it be, for those old creeds were forged in the furnace of persecution, and tempered by the cold blasts of adversity—and they did good service in their day. Still must we fight ; still do we need a shield invulnerable to the new weapons of our ancient foes. Like the Prince Arthur of the Faerie Queene, with his buckler of a diamond, would we be " clothed on " with light as with a garment, and ride triumphant through opposing hosts. But whence comes this resplendent warrior among us— in what divine panoply does he advance to victory ?

In the last great Resurrection we are told that what is sown in death shall be raised a *spiritual body*. That spiritual body, " whereof we all are members," is Christ. The Reconciler, wherein divine and human

meet.   It needs no more words, no explanations.
Let there be an end to vexing discussions concerning
the nature, the standing of Christ.   The old things
have passed away—this is the new heaven and the
new earth, and yet eternal, for Love was from the beginning !   The ineffable glory has beamed forth on
us through a human form—the All-Powerful is the All-
Pitying God.   The purest philosophy is reconciled to
the most human needs, and the font of life is near to
every thirsty soul that will approach and drink.
Thro' Him who taught the uttermost of love in death
on Calvary, the divine is brought close to the yearning human ; and through Him who " rose on the
third day," is the human lifted to know its part in the
divine and the immortal.   In the personality of Christ
the two wants meet—worship and life are blended into
one.   The far-off glory of the Eternal is brought near
to human sight and love ; and the limitations of the
finite are gradually burned away by the purifying fire,
in whose ever-ascending flame the affections are uplifted toward their source.   What is a philosophy,
though built on truth itself, without the motive
power of love ?   What is a faith, though passionately
steadfast, without the pole-star of calm Reason in its

cold, changeless heaven? Jesus Christ, born two
thousand years ago in Bethlehem, lives still, and daily
is crucified in every Golgotha where sin sits ravening
amid the bones of death. Shall we deny him, who
has not denied us? Shall we refuse to acknowledge
him as Lord and Master—aye! and in the fullest sense
of obedience and reverence? Shall we dare to say
that we have got beyond him, and reap the fruits of
the harvest he watered with his blood, while we feign
to serve the Master of the vineyard, who sent him to
us as his Son? If we believe in him, let us acknowledge him, freely, fully, fearlessly. If any words, em-
bodying such truth, are creed, by such creed am I
bound. I want no further doctrine, nay, I entreat no
statement may be added, lest some may fancy liberty
of thought impeded. I would not fright away one
earnest inquirer from the fold—but the fold is that of
the Good Shepherd. Reason as you will, philosopher,
with what intellect God has given you, but remember
there is one place for your *heart* to be! Dream as
you will, O poet, but know that Truth is one with the
incarnate Love! Realize for once within you that
Presence of mingled majesty and beauty, and then cast
aside, if you can, that one profession of faith—but not

till then, but not till then ! And while that communion
of spirit is above you—as it is yet in its perfection beyond us all—cling to the standard as a pledge of
victory, and doubt yourself, but not your cause !

" Whosoever will confess me before men, him will
I also confess before my Father which is in heaven."
And let us remember, that though He was angry
with those disciples who rebuked a man " because he
followeth not us," while he uttered in righteous indig-
nation those sublime words of toleration—" He that
is not against us is on our part," yet it is recorded,
" He was casting out devils *in thy name !* "

July 16, 1870.

JOURNAL.

January 19*th*, 1871.—I do not think I shall keep a
journal any more—I want to forget myself. It is *self*
that suffers—out of self is peace. And " he that loseth
his life shall find it." Glorious thought, for there the
strange circle is complete : first, as children we are unconscious of ourselves ; then, we grow into self-knowl-
edge, and we are *men*, and " walk as gods, knowing

good and evil ;" and then comes the higher state, above
ourselves, out of ourselves—not self-consciousness,
but God-consciousness. So are we again as little children. Eden, the world, Paradise—the old story, in
the old Book. Yet have we gained nothing ? was the
conflict nothing ? is Heaven but that first garden ours
again—no more ? Shall we be as never having suf-.
fered ? God forbid ! The Messiah's crown was not
of gold, but thorns—the Messiah's glory "as of the
Lamb, once slain !" I saw in Naples a picture of the
little child asleep upon the cross, its tiny arms embracing with a touching innocence the instrument of
future anguish. If the nails had been thrust then
through the tender baby-feet would the guileless sacrifice have saved the world ? Nay, though the Father's
own hand had struck the blow, and the little one,
seeing His smile, had trusted to the last ! It was the
Man of sorrows, and *acquainted* with grief, who was
tempted in the wilderness, who prayed the cup might
pass—who was " lifted up," that He " might draw all
men unto Him ! " Oh, that being so drawn, *we* might
be " lifted up ! " Self-forgetfulness—the sublime lesson of the cross, the fulfilment, in a wonderful paradox,
of the greatest lesson pure philosophy could teach :

"Know thyself!" Self-forgetfulness—but there must first have been a *self* to *forget!* So nothing is wrong —the unrest, the aspiration, the self-assertion, the self-despisal, all the pain and the harassing consciousness when the soul is waking up, and stretching its wings uneasily. I believe it is all meant—a phase of growth, and some time the poor little breaking buds will blossom into the white flowers of Peace.

It is to me peculiarly touching—this way in which the struggle finds its completeness—this ending where we began, as little children, of whom "is the kingdom of heaven!" How one longs for the baby-days sometimes!

But infinitely better is the last state than the first. There is a sublimity in this innocence which is not of Eden. Purified in the river of the water of Life, absorbed in God, floating in the ocean of His love, to breathe, feel, live in Him—that is Heaven. Neither so shall we lose our own identity. *He in us*, and also, *we in Him*. Not only loved, but *loving* too, and living most perfectly in that. Again I come to that thought —" He that loseth his life shall *find it*."

January 20th.—I wrote part of this yesterday, not

meaning to get so deep, but I think it is going to be a pleasure to me to express sometimes, as far as I can, a thought. Sometimes there is one that haunts me till I put it down in words—or at least measure my strength with it, till I know how much too great it is for me. Sometimes, too, there is a fancy, or a turn of words, that perhaps there is no harm in my catching before it flies. In the midst of duties, so different, which now I am called upon to perform, it may be that in this way now and then I may remember to bring a little oil to my intellectual lamp,—for certainly nothing helps one so much to ideas as trying to express those one already has!

But I talk about this as though I had made a plan, after long reflection, whereas it was but the day before yesterday that the longing to write first came to me. Even now I feel a kind of pain at my heart, which warns me how near is the old habit of introspection. I cannot bear it,—I must not. Oh, Father in heaven! I have given my grief to thee! Keep it for me, till I am strong enough to look at it! Some day thou wilt transmute it utterly into a joy—but, I think, not until we are beyond the River shall we be able to receive it so!

May's bird is singing in my studio while I write.
The darling! Soon I mean to have some plants there
—a hanging basket, and some ferns growing out of a
white shell that Katie gave me, and he will like that.
Now he is very lonely in there, with only the poor little
pictures standing about, waiting till I get the room
ready for painting in. I don't know whether I ever
shall paint much, but I am going to attempt it as soon
as the bare walls shall no longer disconcert me. Last
summer I formed a lovely plan, and now I want to
carry it out exactly as I told Mamma. Everything in
my life is sacred through her now—for everything in
my life was shared with her!

Last May a few pages I had written at Dr. Bellows'
request, were printed in " Old and New," and late in
the summer I received, unexpectedly, a check for
fifteen dollars, the first money I ever made, and as an
earnest of what I had done, it was very pleasant to me.
I remember the glee we had over it, oh, how well! I
had some projects, but was not allowed to give it away;
so at last my wishes gathered about the ideal statue
which has so long reigned over my artist-dreams, and
a cast of the Venus of Milo I must have! May and I
went in search of it on Wednesday, and the lovely

white thing came home the next evening. I bought
also Michelet's beautifully illustrated book "L'Oiseau,"
wherein I have glimpses of the free Nature-world of
wings and song. With that and the master-piece of
antique Art to contemplate, I ought to be happy—out
of my "fortune." One thing more I have, a mask of
Michael Angelo's Dying Captive. That, in its incom-
pleteness, is but a suggestion,—yet it has in it for me
all Italy, coming beautifully between the others, and a
never-to-be-forgotten remembrance of last summer's
happy reading !

These things are the beginning of my studio. The
Venus is to stand in a niche, lined with some warm
dark color, and sheltered behind the folds of a rich
green curtain (my only piece of luxury), which is to be
drawn aside, revealing the *genius loci*. Then I shall
have rugs on the floor, and some time a pretty wood-
carpet. I have a good many studies to put on the
walls, and my own pictures ; it is a question if I shall
not get very tired of seeing them every day ! About
all these I mean to twine Autumn leaves, and wreaths
of that graceful Hartford fern which Rosalie Goodman
gave me ; and long trailing pieces of gray Southern
moss, a present from Zelina Ripley. My mantel is to

be draped, a shelf and a bracket or two put up, and
then with my green growing things in the window, and
May's bird, I shall have a little bower of my own to
paint in. I like to think of it now, and it is good for
me to think of it!

February 3d (Friday).—At the Philharmonic to-day.
There is a musical silence, and there is a silence that
is only absence of sound. In some symphonies there
comes a crash, and then a dead feeling of vacancy.
That is one silence. But let a master wield the
mighty mass of instruments—there comes a rushing
wind, and the great waves of sound pile up into a
mountainous *crescendo*, then a breathless pause, and
the sky bends low to hear the coming murmur of the
thunder! Or in the midst of rippling melodies, well-
ing up in floods of living sunshine from the warm full
heart that has beat near to Mother Nature's, there
falls a sweet hush of peace, and the waters gather into
some still pool, deep with heaven's depths of azure,
tranquil as though it never would overflow the brink
of its own perfectness.

But these words do not show forth those silences.
In their own nature they are inexpressible, and being

beyond words, we look on them with awe. What is this something ultimate, this ocean which surrounds and encloses sound, yet penetrating into it and defining it with subtle walls of boundary? Penetrated in its turn by the invisible echoes of spent music, our conception of it recedes into the farthest limits of space; yet it is about us, intimate as the air, and as necessary to sound, of which it is the background, as shadow is to sunlight. Do we not think of silence as enveloping creation during that mysterious brooding of the Spirit, and broken only with those words that, bringing Light, struck the first chord of the harmonious universe, and set the spheres in motion?

There is a silence of life, and there is a silence of death—a blank, a hopelessness, a chill—but of that I shall not speak. Little do we know now of what may follow either; little do we know now of the great Composer's plan; but we have in the grand symphony *our* instruments, and if sometimes our discords are but the steps to a more glorious height of harmony, may we not also bear the weary pauses with a sure hope that they, too, work to music?

February 8th.—May's bird was singing to-day his

very sweetest, after a long time of quietness—and what
has stirred his little soul to melody ? In my studio the
men were sawing the wood-carpet, and he needs must
turn the harsh sound of their tools to song ! What a
transmutation ! Lead to gold was nothing to it !
Birdie, you are a little philosopher—or better, perhaps !

February 10*th.*—My studio is finished, and most
lovely it is. How it would have satisfied Mamma !

February 12*th.*—For days this week there has been a
superabundant electricity in the air, such as we often
notice in winter, but lately it has been constant.
Usually a spark, when hands touch, is noticed as
something to be spoken of, and the little *crackle*
makes the children laugh. But now, as they run to
kiss me, there is no sound, only a sharp flash of pain
runs through the centre of the sweetness. I do not
think they know it, the dear little ones ! But it has
given me a strange, mystical notion concerning love
and love's intensity. The bitterness that points the
arrow of the joy, the piercing underneath the softness,
the fire in the midst of the kiss !

The more we love, the more we are able to suffer ;

and in love's self there is the inner ache of longing. But would we part from that to escape from this? Nay, a thousand times! And I think of one thing more. That sudden, silent flame, which we knew only by the pain of it, may it not be the emblem of the spirit? I know of nothing more like spirit than this impalpable, imponderable essence, which pervades all nature with its mysterious vitality—Electricity, running through the universe on the messages of the Unseen, winged with the silent, unutterable powers of Light and Heat. Not the secret of Life yet, but marvellous type of a mystery ineffable!

February 18*th.*—Last night they were talking of the weight of the atmosphere upon a square inch of the human frame, and the tremendous consequent pressure upon the whole body, while yet we move so freely and so lightly upon our daily errands, unconscious of, because interpenetrated with, the enwrapping force. It flashed across me: Is not this the "perfect law of liberty?" The sublime paradox of the New Testament—the new liberty fulfilling, not destroying, the old law? It is the Spirit which, filling, vivifying the universe, makes—is—Law, constraining, crushing where there is a void, if so be it may force its way through broken stone, through bruised flesh, into the heart of an emptiness that knows not yet the presence of its life-bringing breath ; but gentle as an angel's touch upon the brow of one who, filled with the Divine inspiring, moves in his own element, and, God being in him, need not be afraid to be in God !

March.—I scarcely dare touch on this : The innocent suffering for the guilty.   It is a mystery that goes down deep, close to the infinite heart of God. How deeply it searches into some human hearts, He only knows.   But the answer is in the purification by pain—purification of the *sufferer*—that seems not so hard to understand : though its anguish be as of death sometimes, and blinding in the poignancy of it, still it is comprehensible, and received as truth in clearer moments ; but the purification of those *suffered for*, that is the inner of the innermost.   But certainly between the guilty and the One infinitely pure there must be some reconciling link, and that is in the suffering innocence of a loving *mediator*.   I wish the word were not incrusted with such a husk of dogmatism. One *standing between*, not to avert judgment, but to win from sin—not to intercede with the Father, but to implore the child. The Father loves already— did He not send His Son ? But the child—oh ! how it needs to know that love, and, knowing it, to hate the sin that makes it suffer! A goodness, perfect though it might be, that could pass serene through a world of guilt and pain, might comfort, might alle- viate, but it would never save ! That mysterious bond of anguish was the only one that could connect the sinless with the sinning. It has come to me in a wonderful illumination—Life asking, half answering the question, and the Story, with its perfect type, nay, with the human, divine reality fulfilling all. It is a mystery, but not a contradiction ; underneath reason, but not against it. There is no avenging God, but One who loves beyond all we "can ask or think." Yet who loves so much as the sinless, who can be truly merciful but the truly just ? Oh, Christ dying is no dogma, but a living, breathing truth. "Greater love hath no man than this, that a man lay down his life for his friend." At the root of love's bliss lies the pain of love's sacrifice, and the "shedding of blood" is the "healing of the nations." To suffer,

12

then, is blessed beyond all words—to give is to be
rich beyond all counting. Suffering, we rejoice, yet
not for ourselves; giving, we gain, yet for others
more! Oh, blessed baptism which Christ was bap-
tized with! Oh, sacred cup which Jesus drank! Oh,
solemn sacrament of blood and of fire, we "know not
what we ask." The flesh trembles, the spirit faints,
but He, beyond what we can ask or think—He gives
"exceeding abundantly." He gives—the crowned
king! He gives, the Lamb who died! We ask for
thrones, He gives a cross! We seek ourselves, yet
has He not given us Himself? O yearning, waiting
love! O gentle Saviour, to men's eyes abased in
that strange "lifting up," shalt thou not draw all men
unto thee? And following, though far off, in thy
steps, shall not we, to whom thou hast vouchsafed
the grace to bear in their own cross some shadow of
the weight of thine—shall not we, unworthy as we
are to be partakers of the suffering, be partakers also
of the consolation!

June 3*d*.—How many thoughts there are in us,
growing up, so we can feel them stirring and pushing,
and yet, somehow, the garden is all shut up, and if
anybody goes by, there is a great high fence of *silence*

between them and it ! Well, they want to get uttered
—the poor thoughts—and I suppose that is the reason
they strive so under the dark ground, that is very
warm and kind to them, I know, and *gives* them
something, too—almost all, perhaps—though they
don't know it, struggling on through the dimness,
feeling the heaviness about them, and the clog, they
think, though all the time it is the very flesh and
blood their aspiring little selves are made of! Then,
some time, they come up. They are close to our
lips, and shine out of our eyes, and we know they
are, by the looks and the perfume of them. But suppose we try to touch them,—how they shrink and
shiver, and make up little wrinkled faces at us, and we
think they are going to die, in the fading and the
paleness of their fairy-like reluctance ! Yes, try to
write a thought down, and it is as hard to catch as a
south wind, or a butterfly ! Then, too, you feel as if
you were not doing right—as if the pretty blossom
ought to be left growing in its shady nook, undis-
turbed in the midst of the crowding and the tangle of
its sister-growths in the wildwood. Shall we dig it
up, and shake its tender roots, and carry it out into
the sunny broadness of the garden ? Let them alone,

most of them, for they are not strong enough for the
transplanting, and the clinging tendrils would break
if you untwined them.   Let them stay there in their
solitude, where no eye sees them, even a loving one,
that could distinguish a rare blossom from among the
lowly undergrowth of clustering sweetness!   Perhaps
a nameless odor may steal up behind the envious wall
that hides them from the highroad, and gladden so,
unseen, a weary passer-by!

Yet transplanting is good, too, for some things, and
gives a room for larger growth.   Well, we shall see.
Seed-time must be, and harvest also!   But the har-
vest-days need not be very near—to be sure of them!

June 7th.—Poets and little children are never afraid
you will not understand them.   They have their hearts
full, and they speak—as a bird sings—for the thought's
sake, and not for the world's.   But with a touching
confidingness to the world they go—for they must
have somebody to tell.   They can't explain—their
story "says itself" in their own baby-speech, and
they must trust you for the rest.   A little bit out of
heaven, perhaps, they have to bring you, a morsel of
sky in a blue flower-cup, or a star caught twinkling in

a scrap of dingy quartz ; but it is a weed or a stone to you—so far off from the childlikeness. Your loss too ; but the sorrow is the little one's, and it runs away grieved, because you do not understand—happy if it has its mother's lap to hide its tears in !

June 17th.—I gave Nora a bird yesterday. It is very young yet, and does not sing ; but she is so happy, loving it already for the sake of the song that is to be ! It seems to me it is like God's gifts to us, this winged thing, with a secret of glad ˙voice hidden in its tender breast—a possession, hardly yet a *having*—something to hold and cherish, something entirely ours, yet not all ours at once. In all God's giving there is a withholding, yet what he withholds is, in the very promise, given, and the waiting—may not that be a very sweet part too ? " For all is yours —things present, things to come." All *is*, not even *will be*. Surely, the promise is in our hand, and though the beauty be not yet all unfolded, it is *given*— let us be sure it is received.

June 18th. (From a letter to Z. R.)—Do you know the Adagio of Beethoven's XI. Sonata ? Do play it,

and think of me !   It says something for me. . . . .
I should be vain to say my thought were worthy of
such a garment, but it is an ideal purple robe that it
might wear, if it were crowned !—I am getting mystical ; but you and I pledged friendship on an ame-
thyst, and I want you to see in this musical coloring
the alternate glow and deepening of the waves of
red and blue—the passion and the peace—that unite
at last into the spiritual rapture, the tremulous, soft
glory of the culminating purple.